Pietro Aretino's Dialogues

Book One

A MODERN TRANSLATION

BY

ULTAN BANAN

'What pornography is really about, ultimately,

isn't sex but death.'

Not a lot needs to be said to preface the *Dialogues,* which is why this will be short. But since the import of Pietro Aretino to the world of contemporary arts remains uncharted, this introduction is perhaps necessary.

Pietro Aretino was a wordsmith. A pornographer. A playwright. He was a hustler too. After a riotous youth in Perugia he moved to Rome, where he shacked up in the mansion of a rich old hedonist called Agostino Chigi, who kept a harem of young lads whose main purpose was the entertainment of rich old men. Aretino was one of those lads, who peddled their arses for access to high society. No doubt he rubbed up against a few cardinals while at the mansion; it was a notorious party place for the Roman elite.

It was here he got his first break in the arts. It is said he was involved in various projects of the artist Raphael, and it was Raphel's apprentice, Julio Romano, with whom Aretino would later create the world's first work of commercial pornography.

Shakespeare, we know for sure, was intimately familiar with the work of Julio Romano – he even mentions him by name in *The*

Winter's Tale. What also seems possible, however, is that Shakespeare was a fan of Pietro Aretino's work.

Considerable (too many to be mere coincidence) parallels exist between Aretino's play *The Courtier* and Shakespeare's *Twelfth Night*. And since Shakespeare liked to 'draw heavily from the Italian well', it is almost certain he read Aretino. And, we can surmise, loved it.

And that is all I'm going to say on his history.

Pietro Aretino was a literary pioneer. In an era when most works of Italian literature were penned in Latin, Aretino chose to write in the common Italian tongue of his day. It is this fact more than anything else that has inspired this interpretation. For to be fully appreciated, Aretino should be read in a language that speaks to the modern reader, for the profanity, the blasphemy, the irreverence and the comedy, do not come across fully without it.

Perhaps in this day and age, when we have seen, heard and done everything, the *Dialogues* does not have the same impact. But one fact is true and will remain always so: Aretino's Dante-like depiction of sixteenth-century Rome was the first true work of comedy–pornography. And to date, no one has done it better.

Pietro Aretino's Dialogues

Book One

HERE BEGINS

the first day of the whimsical Dialogues of Pietro Aretino,
in which, under a fig tree outside Rome,
Nanna educates Antonia on the life of Nuns.

Antonia — Look at the long face on ya, Nanna. Not really fittin a woman who has the world at her feet.

Nanna — The world, you say?

Antonia — The world, aye. Leave the worryin to me, who can't even raise a bark from a dog. I'm poor but proud, and if I made a hussy of myself then the Holy Spirit would hardly raise an eyebrow.

Nanna — Antonia, everyone has their troubles. Where you think there's joy, there is only misery, and so much of it you wouldn't believe. I'm tellin ya, that's the way of the world.

Antonia — Aye, so it is—but for me, not for you. You have the best of everything. In the squares, in the taverns—everywhere!—all you hear is 'Nanna this' and 'Nanna that', and your house is always mobbed. All of Rome parades through it as if it were carnival.

Nanna — Aye, true. All the same, I'm not happy. I'm like a bride with a full larder, who even though she's famished doesn't dare eat. I'm tellin ya, love, my poor heart is wrecked. Christ save me.

Antonia — Ah, Nanna. The woes are sittin heavy on ye.

Nanna —Patience. You'll see for yourself.

Antonia — Ach, stop—you'll only tempt fate.

Nanna — You think I'm puttin it on, do ya? Now that my wee girl has turned sixteen, I have to decide what to do with her. Everyone's on my back. One says to me, 'Make her a nun and give us another saint'; the next says, 'Get her hitched. Anyway, you're loaded, so you won't miss what the wedding costs ye'. Another tells me to make a whore of her: 'The world is rotten anyway', they say, 'and by making her a courtesan you'll make her a lady. With all what she makes and what you have already you'll soon be a queen'. They're drivin me nuts. See what I'm sayin? Even for Nanna there's trouble.

Antonia — Some troubles you have, Nanna. All seems sweet to me. You sound like a woman who spends the day gettin pampered then complains the powder makes her chuff itch. Real trouble is seein the price of bread go up, seein the wine scarce, havin to pay the rent, or bein struck down with some ague and not being able to rid yourself of the pain. Troubles? You're havin a laugh.

Nanna — Why you bothered anyway?

Antonia — Because you were born and bred in Rome—you should be able to handle this with your eyes shut. Tell me this, weren't you in the convent?

Nanna — Aye, I was.

Antonia — And weren't you married too?

Nanna — Sure you know I was.

Antonia — And didn't you do a spell of whorin?

Nanna — I did. Still do.

Antonia — So of all three, surely you can say which is best.

Nanna — Oh Mother of God, no.

Antonia — Why not?

Nanna — Because today nuns, wives and whores live a different life. It's not like it was before.

Antonia — Ha ha! Life has always been the same everywhere—people eat, they drink, they sleep. They go here and there, they listen, they watch. Men have always pissed standin up, we women take a more unhurried approach. So go on, tell me somethin about the life of nuns, wives and whores of your day. I swear to Christ, I'll tell ya what to do with your daughter in a heartbeat. First, go on and tell me why makin her a nun has you all stressed.

Nanna — Aye, alright.

Antonia — Go on and give it to me—I've enough bread and wine here for three days. And anyway, today's the feast of Magdalene and we've sod all else to do.

Nanna — You sure?

Antonia — Aye. Get on with it.

Nanna — Fine. Today I'll tell you all about the life of a nun. Tomorrow I'll tell you what it is to be a wife, and the day after all about bein a whore. Sit down. Make yourself comfortable.

Antonia — I'm fine here. Go on.

Nanna — First off, I feel like cursin that auld dog of a Monsignor. He was the one who pulled out the thorn, if you get my meaning.

Antonia — Are you gonna get all wound up on me now?

Nanna — Antonia, love, being a nun, a wife or a whore is like comin to a crossroads—you're left there wonderin which way to set foot, and before you know it the Devil pulls you off down the worst way. It was the Devil himself was in my old man the day he dragged me off to the convent, even against my mother's will, God bless her. Aye, there was a woman. You probably know the woman she was.

Antonia — I heard she performed miracles in a house out back of the Via dei Banchi. Also that your father, who was a police informer, married her outta love.

Nanna — Christ, don't bring that up. Rome wasn't Rome anymore, once they were gone. Anyway, gettin back to the story... It was early May when Mona Manetta—that's was my mammy's name, but they called her 'Sweet Tina'—and Ser Barbieraccio, my auld fella, after they'd got all the relatives together, uncles and aunts, cousins and nephews and brothers, the whole herd of em, they led me to the convent dressed all in silk and with the crown of virginity on my head, a golden headdress with roses and violets, and with perfumed gloves and velvet slippers; if I remember correctly, the pearls on my neck and the gown had belonged to Pagnina, who'd just entered the order.

Antonia — Of course they did.

Nanna — All dressed up to the high nines, I entered the church. There were thousands in there, they all turned round to see me come in. One auld fella said: 'What a beautiful bride she'll make our Lord!', and another: 'What a pity to make such a beautiful girl a nun!' Others blessed me, others drank me in with their eyes, another said: 'You'll make some dirty friar very happy'. I didn't know what he was on about then. Then I heard some very beastly sighs. I knew it was a lover of mine, who never stopped gurning all through the mass.

Antonia — You filthy cat—you had lovers before you were a nun?

Nanna — Who wouldn't have? But there was no ridin. Anyway, I was seated in front of the other women and after a while they started singin the mass. Then they put me on my knees between my mother and my aunt Ciampolina, and there was a bit of organ music. After the mass, the priest blessed my habits which were on the altar, and when the gospel was said they lifted me up and made me kneel before the altar. Then the priest sprinkled me with holy water and sang the *Te Deum Laudamus* with the others, and all the other hundred bloody hymns, and I was stripped of my gown and clothed in the holy habits. Everyone crowded in, all moaning and groaning like in a stampede.

Antonia — Mayhem. I can just imagine.

Nanna — When the ceremonies were done and they'd given me the benediction, a door opened, squeaking like the lid on the poor box. I was lifted to my feet and led to the door. Twenty nuns and the Mother Superior were waitin for me, and soon as I saw her I gave a curtsy and she kissed me on the forehead, then said I-dunno-what to my mammy and daddy and all the family. They were all sorrowing like children. Then the door slammed behind me and there was a great wail.

Antonia — Where was the wailin comin from?

Nanna — From my poor lover. The very next day he became a friar, or so they told me.

Antonia — What a sack of misery.

Nanna — The door slammed shut so quickly it practically skelped my arse on the way through. I didn't even have the chance to say goodbye. I felt like I was bein buried alive. I swear, I was expectin to see all these women half-dead from chastity and fasting. God, I cried. I went into the refectory with my eyes glued to the ground. My heart was in my throat. When I got there a whole host of sisters rushed to hug me. I lifted up my eyes to see. I couldn't believe it—all those fresh and happy faces! I was thinkin, there's no way these are women of the habit. Then came the friars and the priests, and some laymen mixed in, some of the strongest, happiest, and most handsome young men you've ever seen. Each man took his darling by the hand... I swear, they were like angels come down from heaven.

Antonia — Careful now... You wanna be bringin heaven into your dirty stories?

Nanna — Well then, they seemed nymphs in the throes of love.

Antonia — That's more like it—keep goin.

Nanna — The men took their sisters by the hand and gave them the sweetest kisses in the world. They were even competing to see who could dish out the most honey.

Antonia — And who slipped the most sugar, do you think?

Nanna — The friars, no doubt about it.

Antonia — Really?

Nanna — If you wanna know why, you need to read *The Whore of Venice*.

Antonia — Phew. So what then?

Nanna — Then they all sat down to the most sumptuous feast I've ever seen. In the most honoured place sat the Mother Superior, on her left the Abbot, and behind her the treasurer and the Bachelor of Arms. Beside her, in turn, sat the Master of Novices, then in a line a nun, a monk, and a layman, and at the foot of the table I don't know how many clerics and friars. I was placed between the convent's preacher and the confessor. Then the food came out. I'm tellin ya, love, such a spread the Pope has never eaten the like of. On the first assault the place went silent. I mean, they went at the food like dogs to the bowl, you hear me? Not a word was heard.

Antonia — And this is your first day in the convent?

Nanna — Ha ha ha!

Antonia — What are you laughin at now?

Nanna — I was just thinkin about this shameless friar, God forgive me, the jaws on him goin like two grindstones, his cheeks swollen like a man blowin a trumpet. Puttin his mouth to the bottle and guzzlin the lot.

Antonia — May God drown him.

Nanna — When they were full up, the chattering started up again. I thought I was in the marketplace in the Piazza Navona, surrounded by customers hagglin with the Jews. Then after a break, they went pickin at the chicken wings and the drumsticks, offerin them to each other like swallows feedin their young. And Jesus, the laughter when someone offered up the capon's ass. Christ, that caused an uproar.

Antonia — What a bunch of reprobates.

Nanna — I felt like boking when I saw one nun chewin up a mouthful then taking it out and passin it to her friend.

Antonia — Aw, the dirty witch.

Nanna — Now, after eatin, they all come over a bit melancholy, the way some men do after they get the ride. They started makin toasts. The convent's Holy Father picks up his glass and toasts the Mother, then swallows the wine like sacrament. Everyone now misty-eyed from the drink. Soon they all would've passed out if a handsome boy hadn't just come in. He'd a basket in hand covered with this thin white linen cloth, like snow. No—frost. Or maybe milk. It was whiter than the shine of a full moon.

Antonia — What was in the basket?

Nanna — Easy, don't hurry me. The boy bowed and said: 'Good health to your lordships. A servant of this fine company sends you this gift of the fruits of earthly Paradise.' Then he placed it on the table. There was a burst of laughter—the whole table roared.

Antonia — God, woman, get to it.

Nanna — As soon as the fruits were seen, their hands—and I'm talkin about hands that were already engaged, if you get my meaning, for there was plenty of gropin going on—were all over the basket. I mean, they went at it like pickpockets emptying a purse.

Antonia — Jesus, what fruit was it? Tell me for God's sake.

Nanna — They were those glass fruits they make in Murano near Venice that look like big cocks, except these ones had two big balls that would've put a bull to shame.

Antonia — Ha ha ha! They went for it, huh!

Nanna — And the girl who got the biggest and the thickest, now that was a lucky girl. And not one of em forgot to kiss it, sayin, 'Sacred these little blessings that forestall the temptations of the flesh.'

Antonia — The dirty sows. Devil take em all.

Nanna — And there's me actin like a pure innocent from the country, stealin glances at the fruit like a crafty cat, one eye on the cook and with a paw on the meat. And if it wasn't for the girl sat next to me who took two then gave me one so she didn't look like a pure dirty minx, I would've grabbed my own. When the uproar got too much, the Mother stood up and so did we, then she gave us a swift blessing.

Antonia — Forget the blessing. Where'd you go after?

Nanna — I'll tell you now. We went into this room all covered in paintings.

Antonia — What paintings? Like the penances of Lent or the Stations of the Cross, or something?

Nanna — Penances! Nah, these paintings would've stopped you dead. The room had four walls. On the first was the life of St. Nafissa, the patron saint of whores. There she was, a good girl at the tender age of twelve, all full of charity, handin out her dowry to police spies, card sharps, parsons, footmen and all kinds of chancers. Finally, when she'd nothin left, she sat down all pitiful and humble right in the middle of the Sisto Bridge with nothing but her stool, her mat and her little dog, and a crumpled sheet of paper on top of a reed, which she fanned herself with to keep off the flies.

Antonia — And why was she sittin in the road?

Nanna — She was preparing to go about the work of dressin the naked poor. So young, as I told you, sittin with her head high and her mouth open. You'd have thought she was singin an amorous lament. She was also painted standing up and facing a man who was too ashamed to ask for her little gifts. Still, so sweetly she led him to her tiny cell where she consoled the afflicted; first she took off his clothes, peelin off his pants and uncovering his little pigeon, making such a fuss about it the fellow got carried away with pride and dove between her legs, entering her with the fury of a stallion hopping the mare. But not bein the kind of girl who could look it in the eye, or maybe not wantin to look at it when it was all red and swollen, she turned her back to it like a champion.

Antonia — God bless her.

Nanna — Well He did bless her. She's a saint after all, isn't she?

Antonia — True enough.

Nanna — God, what didn't I see on that wall? There was painted there too the people of Israel, whom St. Nafissa graciously sheltered and always satisfied. And some of them, after havin tasted her pleasures, would walk away fists stuffed with coins that others had forced into her hand. Imagine goin to someone's house for dinner, eating their food and enjoying their wine, then before you leave, they put a coin in your hand to get you home?

Antonia — Bless you, Saint Nafissa! Who's the girl that can follow in her holy footsteps?

Nanna — Everything she ever did is drawn on that wall, even her final moments. At her graveside, you can see painted all the Italians she succoured in this world and that she'll find again in the next. There were more screws in her coffin than there are greens in a May salad.

Antonia — God, I'd love to see those paintings.

Nanna — On the second wall is the story of the mute, Masetto da Lampolecchio. I swear, those two nuns who led him into the hut were jumpin for joy, while the dirty dog, pretending to be asleep, had the big mast on him standin so high his shirt was hoisted up like a sail.

Antonia — Ha ha!

Nanna — What a wild scene it was. And seein the hunger that came over their sisters, another two, instead of tellin the Abbess, joined in. Masetto couldn't take it and tried to drive them away. In the end, the Abbess brought order by inviting the man back for a ride. In the end, his prick was gettin such a flayin that he cried out for mercy. The whole village rushed out to witness the miracle, and the convent was canonised as holy!

Antonia — Ha ha ha!

Nanna — On the third, I think, all the nuns of that order were painted with their lovers next to them, and all their children besides.

Antonia — A good and fitting memorial.

Nanna — The last painting was a depiction of all the ways, shapes and modes of fucking and being fucked. In fact, this is where the nuns take inspiration from when they're settlin down for a roll around with their partners. Like this, there's less chance of being wooden in the sack— you know how some women are, lyin there like boards and without any confidence. Ridin such a woman is like takin your soup without salt, know what I mean?

Antonia — So they need a teacher who'll teach em how to fumble.

Nanna — Oh, there's a teacher alright. She shows the girls how to ready themselves when a man gets such a horn on him he'll be for ridin her anywhere: on a chair, a pallet, over a table or even up a ladder, even down on the cold floor, you know the way he gets. In order to teach the proper postures to those good and holy nuns, the teacher must be as patient as the man who trains a dog. You know, it's easier to juggle than it is to stroke a prick well. You need to know how to do it so that even if he's a bit limp on it, the prick'll stand up good and hard.

Antonia — Really? A teacher?

Nanna — Oh yes. Anyway, the paintings, and the chattering and the joking started to bore us. All the nuns, friars, priests and layman, and the young man with the glass cocks, they all disappeared. Only the Bachelor of Arms was left there with me, and because I was alone and nervous, I kept my mouth shut. He said to me: 'Sister Christina,'— that was the name I was christened with soon as I had the habit on—'it's down to me to take you to your cell. Let's go and redeem your soul through the triumphs of the body.' I wanted to keep him at arm's length, so I said nothin. Then he took me by the hand; I was still holdin the big glass banana, which I nearly dropped. I grinned, and the Bachelor, takin this as a sign, kissed me. Bein the daughter of a good and pure mother, I froze.

Antonia — Lord save us.

Nanna — Then I let him lead me away. What after? He led me to a small room among all the others, with only a thin brick wall that was so badly plastered you could put your eye to it and see what was goin on in the next room. Once inside, the Bachelor had opened his mouth to tell me, I reckon, that my beauty was greater than that of a faerie queen, and all about my soul, my heart, dear blood and sweet life, yak yak yak, all while tryin to manoeuvre me into position on the bed, when there was this *rat-tat-tat*, like a barn door swingin, that everyone in the convent heard. It frightened the life out of us. Everyone pelted outta their rooms, bangin into each other as they dashed about, tryin to hide from the Bishop. That's who it was—the Bishop, the convent's benefactor—rappin on the door and spookin us all. Just as he passed through the dormitory, he almost stumbled into the Holy Mother's chamber, where she was with the Holy Father 'workin on the evening vespers'. Apparently the Bishop had just lifted his hand to knock when a savvy nun threw herself at his feet.

Antonia — What a welcome he would've had if he'd wandered in. Ha ha ha!

Nanna — But fortune took us by the nose, I swear, because no sooner had the Bishop put his rear on a seat—

Antonia — Now you're speakin like a good Christian.

Nanna — ...when here comes the Dean who brings news that the Archbishop's on his way. So the Bishop jumps up and runs off to greet him, ordering us to ring the bells. As soon as he steps out, everyone drifts back to what they're doin, except the Bachelor, who has to leave to kiss the Archbishop's hand on behalf of the Mother Superior. And the rest of them flew back to their lovers like starlings back to the olive tree after bein chased by the farmer.

Antonia — I'm like a baby cryin for the tit, waitin for you to get to the juicy part. Come on, come on—stop peelin the egg and give me the bloody yolk.

Nanna — So, let's get to the point. I was on my own now, and since I'd already made myself available to the Bachelor, I didn't want to go against the customs of the convent and jinx my first night there. I was still holdin the glass prick in my hand, very much like someone gettin their first glimpse of the big nasty billy-club. I was astounded by it and couldn't understand why the sisters had gotten all worked up over it. While I was sufferin this confusion, I heard a burst of laughter that would've cheered a dead man. It kept gettin louder and louder, so I figured I'd find out where it was comin from. I put my eye to a crack in the wall, cause in the dark you see better with one eye than two; so I put my eye to the brick and—

Antonia — What'd you see? Tell me, for the love of God...

Nanna — In a cell were four nuns, the Holy Father, and three milky-white blushing friars, who were stripping the Reverend Father of his cassock and slipping him into a rich satin robe. They put this velvet cap on his head, all adorned with glittering stones and with a huge white plume on top. Then, his sword swingin at his side, the blessed Holy Father started strutting back and forward like cock of the walk. The nuns had taken off their habits and the friars their tunics, and so they switched clothes, the friars puttin on the nuns' habits and the nuns the friars', and one of the nuns put on the Holy Father's cassock.

Antonia — What a bunch of saucy monkeys.

Nanna — Now it gets even better...

Antonia — Why? What happened?

Nanna — Because the Reverend Father called the three friars, and leanin on the shoulder of one of em, ordered him to take out his mickey. So the handsomest of them took the sparrow from the nest and rested it in his palm, and stroked the back of it like he was strokin the tail of a cat. It soon started to purr. Well, that little sparrow rose up out of its nest, so the Reverend Father grabbed the youngest prettiest nun, threw her tunic over her head and pushed her face down into the bed. He pried open her cocoa tunnel with his fingers and had a good ol' look in there, his face with the rapture of the saints on it. Then he contemplated her snatch, which was not too lean and not too puffy, but somewhere in between, and it quivered and glistened like smooth ivory. Her arse cheeks were nicely dimpled, and soft, soft as fresh cotton, and her thighs so smooth that a hand would slide down it like a hand on ice. There was less hair on her than an egg.

Antonia — So the Reverend Father spent the evening in holy contemplation, did he?

Nanna — Oh no. Cause next he took his paintbrush and wet it with a bit of spit, then he slipped it into her colour cup and made the fine little nun twist. And just to be sure he'd drive it home deep, he beckoned his favourite friar behind him who pulled the Father's breeches down to his ankles, fell to his knees and went at his rusty glory with his tongue, and while the Father was hammering away he watched the two other friars who had two of the sisters on the bed and were now dippin their wicks, all to the despair of the last sister. Poor thing, she was so squint-eyed nobody wanted her. Instead she went and filled one of those glass cocks with warm water, sat down on a pillow on the floor, lay back and thrust that big appendage inside her, burying it sword-deep. I swear, the smell of sex comin through the wall got me so wound up that I started rubbin my little beaver like a cat rubs its back against the scratching post.

Antonia — Ha ha! And how did it all finish?

Nanna — When they'd pushed and pulled and squirmed and twisted for a half-hour, the Reverend Father cried: 'Now all you, my dear boys and girls, come and kiss me together—you too, my little dove.' With one hand on an arse cheek and the other on a tight little quim, a strangled look on his face, he kissed this one and kissed that one, and the two nuns and the friars and the one with the tongue up his dirty badge and the one he was ridin, and even the little nun with her Roman tickle-stick, were all writhing and lashing together... and the cries out of em: 'Oh Christ my Saviour!' 'Gimme that sweet tongue!' 'Harder, give it to me!' 'Wait, I'm comin!' 'Deeper I tell you!' 'Holy God!' 'Help!' 'Don't let me go!' and 'Oh Christ, drive it right up me!', and the groans and the whispers... listenin to em you'd have thought they were reciting the scales: *so, la, fi, ma, re, do...* eyes poppin outta their heads, gasps and shakes, twistin and turnin so that the chests and the beds and the chairs and chamber pots shook and rattled like the place had been hit by an earthquake.

Antonia — Holy Jesus...

Nanna — Then from the liver, lungs, heart and soul eight sighs rose up as one. And as they sighed they fell to the floor like drunks. And me, strung out from the pure stress of watchin, I turned away and sat down, and stared at the glass cock on the bed next to me.

Antonia — Wait a minute, hold on—who were the eight you heard?

Nanna — Jesus, don't be so nickety. Just listen.

Antonia — Go on.

Nanna — Lookin at that glass appendage, I came over all hot. I'm tellin ya, what I'd just watched would have excited the holy hermit himself. And just starin at the thing I was seized with temptation... I was like a wild animal. But I didn't have the hot water the sister had used to fill the glass cock, which was necessary to use it. So, all riled up with the horn, I used my wits...

Antonia — But how?

Nanna — I pished in it. Right in the little hole that was made for fillin it with hot water. But why drag out the story? I lifted up my nun's habit and rested the cock on a chest with the hard end of it between my thighs, and I lowered myself, slowly at first. Christ, that really took the edge of my horn. At first it stung and burned, and caused me both pain and pleasure, but soon, drenched all with sweat and ridin it mad like, I bounced so hard on it I nearly had the whole thing up inside me. As it disappeared into my quim, I felt I was dyin a death. With the thing buried in my sweet wetness, it was like I was melting. Then I pulled it out. I still had a mad burning on me, like an itch that has not been fully scratched. But when I looked down at the thing, I saw it was all bloody. I was so frightened I almost cried out: 'Lord, let me confess!'

Antonia — But why, Nanna?

Nanna — Why? I thought I'd done myself an injury! Then I put my hand to my mouth and took it away, and it too was scarlet. I began to cry and pull at my hair. Even more than being afraid of dyin, I was afraid of the Mother Superior.

Antonia — Why's that?

Nanna — I was afraid she'd know the real cause of the blood and lock me away like a harlot. And even if she were only to tell the others about me, don't you think I had somethin to cry about?

Antonia — Ach, stop.

Nanna — Why?

Antonia — Because all you had to do was tell her about the sister you'd seen friggin herself with the glass cock. She'd have forgiven you straight away.

Nanna — Maybe if the nun had been all bloody like I was. No, in reality, Nanna was in a bit of a fix. As I sat there cryin, there was a bangin on my cell door. So I got up and dried my eyes, and when I opened the door I saw they were callin me to dinner, even though I'd been gorging myself all mornin like a Hun. But since the sight of blood had killed my appetite, I said I wanted to fast that evenin. And securing the door with the broom handle, I stood there trembling with my hand on my muffin. But now that the blood had stopped I didn't feel so bad, and to kill the time I went back to the crack in the wall where there was light glinting through, cause since it was night the sisters had lit a lamp. I put my eye to the crack. Now they were all naked. Soon enough the Reverend Father took his favourite boy, the lanky one, and told him to get up on the middle of the table where the four wicked nuns were eatin. And after makin like he was blowing on a trumpet, the friar cried out: 'The great Sultan of Babylon makes it known to all ye jousters of worth to now take their lances in hand, and he who scores the most targets will be presented with a smooth and hairless ring which he can turn to his enjoyment all the evening long. Amen!'

Antonia — What a fine announcement. His master must have penned it for him. Keep goin, Nanna.

Nanna — Now all the jousters line up for the sport. They take that dark little squinty nun who's been stuffin herself with the glass cock, and bend her over and paint a target round her arse. Then they draw lots. The first shot fell to the trumpeter. He took his run up, spurring himself on with his fingers up his bumhole, then he drove his lance into her quim right up to the hilt. That one thrust was like the work of three. He got a good round of applause for his effort.

Antonia — Ha ha!

Nanna — The Reverend Father had the next shot, so he lined up and took his run, and in turn ran his javelin up the friar's hole, just as the friar had impaled the nun, and there they were all crammed tight together, like a salami between two bits of bread. The third shot fell to one of the nuns, and cause she didn't have a jousting stick of her own, she took a glass one, and with her first shot buried it deep in the Reverend Father's bungle. Then, just for the hell of it, she squeezed the balls of it into her cooch.

Antonia — She musta had a big hefty growler on her.

Nanna —Then the second friar, whose turn it was, drove forward and hit the bullseye. The next nun, copying her sister, took another glass cock and drove it into his hole. When he felt it go in he started squirming like an eel. Then the last two. I got a good giggle when the nun buried her own glass cock in to her sister's slit, and the friar that came last thrust his dipping stick into her chocolate pot... I swear, they looked like a big man kebab roasting on Satan's spit.

Antonia — Ha ha! What a feast!

Nanna — That little squint-eyed nun was havin the time of it, crackin off jokes while the rest of them pumped and squirmed—when I heard her I laughed out so loud they must've heard me. I ducked away. Then I heard squabbling, and when I went back to the crack in the wall it was covered with a sheet, so I couldn't see the end of the clash. I don't know who won the prize.

Antonia — Aw... you let me down, right at the loveliest moment.

Nanna — I was let down too, sweetheart. The feast was closed to me now. But I'm tellin ya, while I was cursin myself for laughing, which lost me my place at the spectacle, I heard again—

Antonia — What'd you hear? Tell me quick...

Nanna — You know, I had the view of three cells, not only one.

Antonia — Holey walls, eh? There's more leakage than a sieve in this place.

Nanna — I don't think the sisters took too much care covering them. In fact, I think they enjoyed watchin each other. Anyway, I hear this wheezing, a sighing and grunting, then a rasping, which seemed to come from about ten people. I listened carefully—it was right at the wall, across from where they'd been jousting—and I could hear whispering. So I got right up to the wall, findin another chink there, and peeked through. And would you believe it? There's these two plump little nuns, legs high in the air with the heavy white thighs quivering like curdled cream. The two of em were workin away with a glass prick. One of em says to the other: 'This is nuts—we can't satisfy ourselves with these useless pokers. They give no kisses, they have no tongues or hands to push our buttons. We need ourselves some flesh and blood. We'll waste our youth fiddlin around with these hunks of glass.' 'You know what, sister,' the other says, 'you're right. You should come with me.' 'Where do you wanna go?' she says. The other lowers her voice to a hush: 'I plan to make a break for it outta here to Napoli. I've a young man there. He has a friend that's perfect for you. Let's get out of this hole and enjoy our youth as all women should enjoy it.' The friend was a saucy little minx and didn't need to be asked twice. They flung their glass cocks against the wall and there was a great shattering. Then they jumped outta bed, packed away their clothes and left the cell. But right after that I heard the sound of slapping, and somebody crying 'Lord save me!', then the sound of scratching and hair being ripped out, and clothes... all very strange. I didn't know what to make of it. But when I brought me eye to the crack, I saw the Mother Superior, who was lamenting and tearing her habits.

Antonia — The Mother Superior?

Nanna — The pious Mother herself, our protectress!

Antonia — What was wrong with her?

Nanna — So far as I could see, her confessor had been pure murderin her.

Antonia — How'd it come about?

Nanna — It went down somethin like this: They were deep into a ride, she was wet and right dyin of the lust, her pussy soakin, when he pulled his cucumber from her salad garden cause he wanted to stick it in her mucky shrubbery, so the poor woman got down on her knees and begged, by the stigmas, by the sorrows, by St. Julian and by the three Magi and the Star and by the *Santa Santorum*, begged the Judas to stick it in her, but he wouldn't. Like a snake, he whacked and bullied her until she turned away, then he made her stick her head in a small stove. Frothing at the mouth he plunged his boaby into her brown eye.

Antonia — The absolute dog.

Nanna — They shoulda hung the scoundrel, cause he took such glee laughin and stickin it in and pullin it out, in out, in out, with a 'tof' and a 'taf', like the sound pilgrims feet make when they get stuck in the wet clay and they lose their slippers.

Antonia — They should've hung, drawn and quartered the bugger.

Nanna — The poor woman, with her head in the stove like that she seemed the very spirit of a sodomite in the mouth of the Devil. In the end the Father, moved by her prayers but with the prick still buried inside her, pulled her head out and carried her on the end of his staff all the way to a stool where he plonked her down and began to go at her like a bull. Then, as if she was disjointed, she bent all the way back searchin for his lips, stickin her tongue out like a cow at the cud, at the same time she trapped his hand in her valise, makin him squirm as if he'd been caught by a pair of pliers.

Antonia — I don't believe what I'm hearin. Every moment somethin new.

Nanna — With that, the holy man spilled his seed. He wiped his prick with a perfumed handkerchief and the Mother gave her snatch a good wipe. Only seconds later they had their arms around each other again, and he said: 'Does it seem right to you my dove, my soul, my heart of hearts, light of my life, that your Narcissus, your Ganymede, your Angel, could not for once have a go at your bunghole?' She replied,

'Does it seem right to you my swan, my falcon, my consolation of consolations, pleasure of pleasures, hope of hopes, that your nymph, your handmaiden, for once could not take your giggle stick as nature intended?' Then she gave him such a bite she left teeth marks on his lips and made him squeal.

Antonia — Good girl!

Nanna — After this, the Mother Superior took his skin flute in hand and put it to her mouth, giving it a little peck. Then she got carried away, and nibbled on it like a puppy chews on your hand, you know the kind of nibbling that makes you laugh and cry at the same time. And the saucy Father went wild, moaning: 'Ah lovely, quite lovely...'

Antonia — The clumsy cat, she mighta taken a bite right outta him.

Nanna — While the good and charitable Mother Superior toyed with her little trinket, there was a very soft tapping at the door of her room. They were startled and had no idea what to do, then they heard a faint whistle. They realised it was the Reverend Father's novice and opened the door at once. The boy knew what they were all about, and the pair of em weren't put out in the least. In fact, the Mother let off playin with the Reverend Father's little birdie and pulled out the novice's tiny tweeter. 'My love,' she said to the Reverend Father, 'will you do me a favour?' 'What's that?' said the nasty Father. 'I want to grate this little stick of cheddar with my grater, but only on the condition that you stick your bum tickler in your novitiate's stink fissure, and if this pleases you, we can go for a right gallop. If not, well, we'll try it another way. We'll find something that works.' Without a second's hesitation, the Father had flung up the sails of the boy's cassock, and seein this, the Mother lay back on the bed and opened her box, and hardly was the boy up on her that she pulled in his stiff little birdie and he collapsed down on top of her, the Father ridin on him like a mule, all of them wriggling in pure delight. She was the first to shoot her load, the others after, and with the game over, they went like wolves at the wine and pastries.

Antonia — How could you control yourself after watchin all that ridin?

Nanna — I was soppin wet after watchin them go to town on the Mother Superior, and I was still holdin that glass diddle-stick in my hands...

Antonia — I bet you had a good sniff at it, like you would sniff a carnation.

Nanna — Ha ha ha! Christ, I had a ragin horn on after all that. So I emptied the cold piss out of the glass cock and filled it up again. Then I shoved it into my muff, and I would've put it right up my arsehole too, just to try everything, you know. You never know what you'll take to.

Antonia — Good on ya. You were just right.

Nanna — I was rubbin the thing over my dirty penny, thinkin about takin the whole lot, weighing up the pros and cons, and my twat was gettin a nice little polishing too from the length of it; I swear, I think I'd have let the dog in the kennel if I hadn't heard the Reverend Father ask leave of the Mother Superior. I rushed over to the wall to hear what was goin on: 'But when will you return, my love, my adoration?' she said. And the Father swore by the litanies, and by the north wind, that he'd be back the next evenin. The boy, who still buttoning up his pants, put his tongue in her mouth by way of goodbye. And as he left, I heard the Reverend Father begin to whisper the vespers prayers.

Antonia — What? The pure charlatan pretending to recite his daily prayers?

Nanna — Uh-huh. As soon as he'd gone, I understood from the departing footsteps that the combat was done for the day, and they were all sallying away to sleep off their victories.

Antonia — Good God Almighty.

Nanna — Now, come here til I tell you this. The two sisters who'd bundled up their clothes had returned to their cell. From what I could hear, they'd found the back door locked by the Mother Superior, and they were proper cursin her out. But somethin came of the attempt, for goin down the staircase they'd found the mule driver there dozing, havin only arrived at the convent an hour or two before. One of them took a shine to him, and said to the other: 'Go on and wake him, and tell him to take some timber from the kitchen and bring it here. You leave it to me. Your sister will soften him up nicely.' The nun did so. But while all this was happenin, I discovered somethin else.

Antonia — What was it?

Nanna — Next to the nuns' room, there was another cell, all decorated up like a courtesan's chamber. In this room there were two divine little sisters. They'd set out a very nice table with a white damask tablecloth, and I could smell lavender perfume through the walls. It was set out lovely for three people, so neatly I can't even describe it. Then they took a whole host of flowers from a basket and arranged them on the table very fastidiously. One of the nuns had placed a garland of laurel in the middle of the table and scattered white and vermilion roses here and there. In the centre of the garland, written out in flower petals, was the name of the Bishop's vicar who'd arrived that very day with his lordship—that's why the bells were tolling and wreckin my ears, and so many stories I missed because of it. So, this wedding feast was all laid out for the vicar, as I found out soon enough. Her companion, meanwhile, threw a nice linen cloth over a bench and set out glasses which were polished up lovely, and put out a pitcher of orange water. At the foot of the bench stood a copper vase, so highly polished you could see yourself in it, and the nun filled it with fresh water. And when all this was finished, one of them took out a loaf and put it on the table. Then they took a rest.

Antonia — You know what, only a nun would have the time to go about settin a table with such diligence.

Nanna — It was almost three o'clock and they were still sittin there when the bell struck. The more impatient of the two shouted out: 'Good God, the Vicar's taking longer than a Christmas mass.' The other said: 'No wonder he's late, sure the Bishop's holding a confirmation tomorrow. He's probably got him doing something or other.' Then they bullshitted for a bit so they wouldn't go out of their minds, but after an hour of this their talk turned sour, and the Vicar was referred to in less affection: 'scoundrel', 'waster', 'pig', were just some of the names I heard him called. Then one nun ran to the fire where two capons were being boiled, and over it a spit on which hung a peacock the nuns themselves had reared. She was for throwin them out the window if only for the other stoppin her. And in the middle of all this kerfuffle, the mule driver, who was on his way to the room of the other two sisters, the ones who'd took a shine to him, took a wrong turn and ended up at the door of our nuns who were waitin on the vicar. The mule driver stumbled inside and dropped the wood on the floor, and the pair of em flew into a rage.

Antonia — And what'd they say?

Nanna — What would you have said?

Antonia — I would've taken fortune by the short and curlies.

Nanna — Which is just what they did. Thrilled at the unexpected arrival of the mule driver, they gave him a king's welcome. Barring the door against his escape, they sat him down and gave him a good wipe down with a towel. The mule driver was about twenty, clean-faced and chubby with a forehead on him like the bottom of a barrel, big and burly and a bit feckless. Sittin there at the table with that delightful spread, he cawed like a monkey and stuffed himself and drowned himself with wine. The two sisters, deprived an age now of the mickey, only sneered at the food. Their hunger was of a different sort. Then the greediest nun, losin her patience, lunged for his lovestick like a vulture. That big galoot would've went right on eatin, but as soon as the hand was on him a big club was pulled from his breeches that would've put any man to shame. It looked like a trumpet. While the one nun was graspin the thing two-handed, the other nun pushed the table outta the way. No sooner was he clear than she straddled him and lifted her habit, and slid down til the big club was between her thighs. She came down on him with her full weight, and soon she was goin at him like the stampede that ensues on the bridge when the Pope's givin his blessing. The chair toppled right over and they fell, the big appendage slippin right outta her meat sleeve, and the other sister, afraid his willy winkie might catch cold, was right down on top of him with her money box. Her companion flew into a rage at havin been robbed of the ride, and went apeshit, grabbin her friend by the throat so fiercely that she threw up. The other turned on her, not even waitin to finish, and the two of the em beat seven bells of shite outta each other.

Antonia — Ha ha!

Nanna — Just as the big ape was standin up to stop the fight, I felt a hand on my shoulder. And a voice: 'Goodnight, my dear little thing.' I was shakin with the fear, especially since I was so lost in what these two horny cats were at. With the hand on my back, I said: 'Oh God, who is it?' I was just about to scream for help when I turned and saw it was the Bachelor who'd left me to see the Bishop. I sighed with relief and said: 'Father, I'm not the sort of girl you think I am... get back now... I'll cry out... God preserve me, God forbid, I'd rather slit my wrists... we can't, never, I say no...' And he said to me: 'How can a little angel like yourself be so cruel? I am your slave, I adore you—you alone are my altar, my vespers, my mass, my fulfilment; if you want me to die, here's the knife, stick it in me. In my heart you'll see only your sweet name written in gold.' And he tried to put into my hand a beautiful dagger with a gilded handle. I wouldn't take it. I kept my eyes to the floor and didn't answer. Then, with the shrill and monotonous insistence of a choir, he broke my will and overcame my resistance.

Antonia — You'd have done worse to kill him—you chose the more pious route. Every self-respecting woman should take your example. Keep goin.

Nanna — Won over by his monkish rambling, in which he told more lies than a broken clock, I let him climb up on me and stick it in me with a *Laudamus Te*, as if he were blessing the palms on Palm Sunday.

His chanting had me bewitched and I let him ride away. What else could I've done, Antonia?

Antonia — Nothin, Nanna.

Nanna — About what I was sayin earlier—would you believe somethin else?

Antonia — What?

Nanna — The fleshy meat stick was less rough and crude than the glass one.

Antonia — What a discovery!

Nanna — I swear by the cross it's true.

Antonia — Why do you need to swear? I believe you every step of the way.

Nanna — Then I pissed, but not really pissing, if you get me...

Antonia — Ha ha ha!

Nanna — This kinda white sticky stuff, like snail slime. He did it three times, would you believe, twice in the old way and once in the modern fashion. And this last way, whoever invented it, I didn't like it one bit. I swear, it was awful.

Antonia — Nah, you got it all wrong.

Nanna — Hanged if I'm wrong. Whoever discovered it musta been bored outta their skull, they couldn't have had the least appetite for it, if not—ah, Jaysus, don't make me say it.

Antonia — Don't write it off altogether. Some people'll kill for it. It's an acquired taste. Ha ha!

Nanna — They can keep it! Now, back to business. After the Bachelor had planted his standard twice in my lady garden and once in my garbage patch, he asked if I'd eaten. From his breath I could tell he was as stuffed as a Jew's goose, so I told him I had. He pulled me into his lap and with one arm around me, fondled my cheeks, my tits, givin me these delicious kisses all the while... I swear, I was rejoicing at the minute and hour I became a nun, thinkin these sisters were livin in true paradise. But suddenly the Bachelor had a notion and decided to take me on a tour of the convent, and said to me, 'Don't worry, we can sleep all day.' I'd seen so many miracles in those four cells, I was sure there were others to see. He took off his shoes and I took off my slippers, and takin his hand I followed him, tiptoeing out of there as if I was walkin on eggshells.

Antonia — Wait, wait—go back.

Nanna — Why?

Antonia — Because you've forgotten those two who were left high and dry with the mule driver.

Nanna — Oh, that's right—I'm daft. In the end, the two poor girls let out their frustrations on the handles of the fire-irons, impaling themselves like criminals on a Turkish spit. One of em was goin so deep with that thing it was nearly comin out her mouth.

Antonia — Ha ha! That's great!

Nanna — Now, I was followin quietly behind my paramour when we came across the cook's little cell, and the eejit had left his door ajar. Glancing in, we saw her foolin around like a bitch in heat with this pilgrim, who'd begged her for alms to go see St. James of Galicia and she'd taken him under her roof. His pilgrim's cloak was folded and set on a chest, and his staff all covered in little icons was restin against a wall, and the two of em were so occupied they didn't even see that the cask was spillin wine all over the floor. Well, we didn't waste any time watchin such a sloppy display, but we went straight to the crack in the cell wall of this nun who'd lost all hope of receiving a visit from her rector, and had flown into such a fury that she'd thrown a rope up over the rafter and had slipped the noose around her neck, and was just gettin ready to kick the stool out from under her when he arrived at the door and pushed his way inside, seein her try to top herself. He shouted: 'What the hell's going on here, do you think I've been cheating on you? Where is your faith?' At these words she snapped out of it and the life flooded to her face, and the rector took her down and laid her on the bed. She gave him a long slow kiss and said: 'My prayers have been answered. I want you to make a dedication to St. Gamignano with the words: '*She commended her soul to God and was delivered.*' And havin said this, she took his meat sceptre in her upright wink, and once he'd a taste for it, came the goat over him and he went on the buck.

Antonia — I wanted to say before but forgot—how about you just stick to 'fuck' and 'prick' and 'cunt' and 'arse'—Christ Almighty, I'd need a degree from Rome to follow you with your 'upright winks' and your 'meat sceptres', your 'lady gardens' and your 'cabbage patches', 'big diddle-sticks' and 'garden leeks', and your 'little birdies' and your 'nightingales', and I don't know what else—'latch in the door' and 'key in the lock', the 'belltower in the Colosseum', the 'mortar', the 'pestle', the 'lance', the 'spear', 'little monkeys', 'parsnips', 'syringes in the flap-valves', fuck knows what else... 'apples', 'pears', 'holy croziers' and 'handles' and 'hafts' and 'happy sticks' and all that other shit. Just say it plain and stop mincin about. Yes means yes, no means no—you got me?

Nanna — Don't you know that debauchery is made all the more beautiful by modesty?

Antonia — Fine. Say it in your own way. Don't get sore at me.

Nanna — Well, in that case, I'll tell you that once he'd had a little taste and got to thrustin his knife proper into the meat, he took his pleasure heartily, thrustin in and pullin out like a madman—ever see the joy a baker's boy takes when he thrusts his fist in and out of the dough? That's the kind of joy our rector was taking. Oh yes, he was really workin her minced pie, pounding the seal into the wax again and again, the two of them rollin from the foot of the bed to the head and back, and on and on. Now it was the sister who was up on him, ridin the rector's ranger, now it was him bearin down into her pink canoe, the two of them shoutin: 'Do it to me!', 'My turn!', and they rolled about so much that the flood walls were finally broken and the sheets flooded, and so they fell apart, she to one side and him to the other, the two of em gaspin for a breath of air. We couldn't keep ourselves from laughin: when he finally pulled out his oar, the rector gave such an explosion of a fart—Jesus, the whole convent shook. If we hadn't clapped a hand over each other's mouths, we'd have been rumbled.

Antonia — Ha ha ha! Jesus, stop and let me get a breath.

Nanna — And as we were sneakin away, we saw the novice's mistress, who was a total little gossip, dragging a filthy porter from under a bed. She was sayin: 'Come out my Hector, my little Trojan, my Orlando, here I am—forgive me for the trouble but I had to hide you.' The rascal lifted up his tattered shirt and waved his piddler at her. She had no trouble understanding. The peasant wasted no time stickin his mickey in her berry bush and made her head spin, and gave her such sweet kisses he made her weep. Not wantin to watch this sweet creature in the hands of such a wastrel, we went off.

Antonia — Where did you go then?

Nanna — To a crack in the wall which showed us a nun who looked like a right Bible aunt, like an Old Testament mother-in-law. I could hardly look at her. She'd about twenty hairs on her head and her scalp was all covered with nits and lice, her face was creased by a thousand wrinkles, and she'd thick bushy eyebrows that covered eyes that were drippin with pus.

Antonia — Some sight you have, if you could see nits on the old woman's head.

Nanna — Just wait. She was drooling, and her mouth and nose were all snotty, and she'd only about two teeth in her mouth, her lips were dry and her chin sharp. A couple of long hairs hung down over her face. Her tits hung like empty ballsacks and her belly—Oh for the love of God—was all shrivelled and shrunken with her bellybutton poking out. And you know what, around her pisshole looked like a month-old cabbage.

Antonia — Even the lowest take care to cover up their shame.

Nanna — Aye, if only. Her thighs were like twigs covered with parchment and her knees were trembling so much she looked like she was about to fall, and, well, you can imagine what the rest of her looked like. The fingernails were like letter openers but all clogged with dirt. So, while we were watchin she bent down to the floor and drew stars, moons, diamonds, squares, letters, and a thousand other things with coal, called out the demons with names that were lost to the Devil himself. Then circling three times around it, she turned her face to heaven and muttered away. Then she took out a wax figurine and stuck a hundred needles in it—if you've ever seen a mandrake, you can imagine what it looked like—and put it close to the fire to roast it, and said these words:

Oh fire, my fire, kill for me,

that cruel man who would flee from me.

She turned the figurine with more fury than they fling bread at the poor house and said:

Itching, itching, burning burning,

Bring my god of love a-running!

The wax figurine was gettin very hot. With her eyes fixed to the floor, she then incanted:

Do demon do, my Joy let him come

Or let the life in him end its run.

After she'd whispered all these verses, lo and behold, someone came knockin at her door, panting and breathless as a man who'd legged it after stealin a bird from the kitchen. The old witch laid aside her magic instruments and opened the door.

Antonia — Buck naked?

Nanna — Aye, in the raw, and the poor man, in the throes of her voodoo and filled with a black hunger, threw his arms round her neck and kissed her with no less passion than he would've embraced Rosa, that legendary courtesan, and sang praises to the old woman's beauty. She chuckled and cried: 'Should these limbs take to bed alone?'

Antonia — Aw, that's just mingin.

Nanna — I won't give you the boke anymore with this old witch.

That's all I know, cause I couldn't watch for another second, and when the bewitched layman, just a pup with barely a hair on his face, plopped her down and got ready to go to work, I turned away. But now for the rest. After that auld witch we went to see the dressmaker, who'd put her master in chains. He was stripped naked and she was kissin him on the mouth, chest, his jiffy stick and his cinnamon ring, just like the wet nurse plops little kisses on the child she's suckling, on its little face, hands, the little body and its lovely little bum, and the dressmaker was as eager to suck at him as the baby goes at the tit. Oh yes, we were ready to see the dressmaker lift her gown, but then we heard a cry, and after a shriek, and then a groan, then there was all kinds of curses that struck terror into our hearts. Dashing to the spot where the noise was comin from, we saw a nun who'd half a baby hangin from her box, pissin out head-first to the relentless farting of the agitated nun. When they saw it was a baby boy, they called the father, the Priest-Guardian. He came accompanied by two middle-aged nuns, and upon arrival he whips out a pen and some paper, and says, 'Let's draw up this baby's horoscope.' And he begins stabbing the paper with the pen until it's covered with a thousand dots and a whole mess of lines and cross-hatching, muttering some gibberish about the house of Venus under the influence of Mars, and when he's done he turns to the party and says: 'Sisters, I hereby inform you that my son, born of my blood and my spiritual heir, will either be the Messiah, the Antichrist, or Melchizedek.' Wantin to get a gander at the hole where the baby had popped out from, my Bachelor tugged at my habit, but I told him I'd seen enough split gashes and I didn't need to see no more.

Antonia — Now you sound more like a nun.

Nanna — Now listen to this. Six days before I arrived at the convent, they'd locked up this young girl who—now, I won't say she was a virgin, far from it, but, how shall I say, was the sort of fleshy maiden only the Lord above can describe. To protect her from some local lord who was in love with her, the Mother Superior kept her in a solo cell, and at night kept the key with her at all times. Well, her young lover, seein that the barred window of her cell looked out over the garden, climbed the wall and, clingin there like a woodpecker, gave her the pecker right through the bars of the window as best he could. The both of em were there clingin to the bars and he was gettin ready to empty his milk in her cup, arms twisted around the bars. And just as he was about to drain his balls, things took a mad turn.

Antonia — In what way?

Nanna — The daft fool had such a fit when he cried out 'I'm coming, I'm coming!', that he let go of the bars and plunged to the roof below, from the roof to henhouse, from the henhouse to the ground, and landed there and broke a leg.

Antonia — Anyway, what was the Mother Superior thinkin? She was expecting the girl to be chaste in a whorehouse?

Nanna — She did it out of fear of the friars, who'd sworn to burn her alive and the whole convent if there was even a hint of mischief. But to get back to the story, the young fella who was thrashin about like a dog, roarin, woke up the whole place and had them runnin to the windows to see what the matter was. They all saw him lyin there in a broken heap. The nuns roused two laymen from their beds and sent em down, and they hoisted him up and carried him away, and I'm tellin ya, this didn't half cause a scandal thereabouts. After this, we went back to our cell in case the day came up with us spyin on the others. On our way we came across a friar, this right greasy prankster who was tellin a tale to a whole mob of nuns, priests and laymen who'd been playin dice and cards all night. Done with the drink, they'd urged the friar to spin them a good yarn. So he goes: 'I'll tell you a story which starts in laughter and ends in tears, and it's about this stud of a dog.' They all fall quiet and he goes on. 'Two days ago as I was passing through the square, I stopped to watch a little bitch in heat, which had about two dozen little dogs after her all drawn to the scent of her snarler, which was all puffed up and so red it looked like a split overripe tomato. They were all having a good sniff at her, and around this little show a mob of kids had gathered to watch this one dog climb up on her and now another one. In order to hide my amusement I put on my frowning monk's face, but the next thing I know, this big unit of a mastiff shows up who looks like a guardian of the underworld. He seizes one dog and flings him to the ground, then takes another and almost rips off its coat. The rest of the dogs scatter in all directions. So the big fella arches his back, his fur bristling like a boar's, eyes wild, grinding his teeth and foaming at the mouth, and he takes after the poor little bitch. After giving her little red button a good sniff, he climbs up on her and gives her two pumps that get her howling, but then, slipping out from under him, she takes off at a run. A few of the other mutts who'd stayed and were standing guard, take off after her too. The big dog, angry now, gave chase. When the bitch saw a crack in a closed door, she dove in and the little dogs after her. The big quasimoto dog stayed outside, for he was so big and mangled he couldn't fit, and stuck outside, he started biting the door and stomping the ground and howling like a dog with the rabies. So after a while one of the little dogs pops out and the big stud jumps right on him and tears off an ear, and the second got it even worse. One by one the mutt took it out on the lot of them, until at the end the blushing bride came out, and without pause he sank his fangs into her throat and throttled her, and then went after all the children who were gathered about, all screaming to heaven as they sprinted away.' And my God, after hearing this, that was it, we didn't wanna hear more. We took ourselves off to bed.

Antonia — Boccaccio won't know what's hit him. He can hang up his boots.

Nanna — I don't know about that. At least my stories ring true. This friar's are a bit embellished, don't ya think? Anyway, didn't I have somethin else to tell you?

Antonia — Keep goin.

Nanna — I got up at noon. My rooster was gone before the crack of dawn, so I went to eat. I had to grin when I saw all those Bacchanalians from the night before. Since I soon got to know them all, it became clear they'd seen me with the Bachelor just as I'd been spyin on them. With lunch over, a Lutheran friar climbed up on the pulpit. He had a thunderous voice, so loud it could've been heard from east to west. He gave the nuns a sermon that would've converted Diana.

Antonia — What'd he say?

Nanna — He said there was nothing more hateful to nature than people wasting their time, because she'd given it to us so she could enjoy seeing her creatures grow and multiply, and above all else, she rejoices when she sees a woman in old age who can say, 'World, go with God—I've had my fun', and more than anything else cherishes the joys of the saucy little nuns, who're like sugar to the Cupid-God, so the pleasures she gives them are a thousand times sweeter than those he gives to the laywomen. Then entering into reasoning about love, about which he covered everything all the way to the flies and the ants, he warned us stiffly that everything that came out of his mouth was straight from the mouth of Truth. Loiterers don't listen as attentively to a busker as those nuns listened to this chatterbox. And after givin the blessing with one of those big glass yokes—you know the one I'm talkin about—he came down and refreshed himself with wine like a horse to water, and went at the pastries like a donkey. He got more gifts than the family of a priest who's just said his first mass, or a mother gives her daughter who's gettin wed. I went back to my cell, and wasn't there long when someone started beatin on the door. I opened it, and standin there was the Bachelor's choirboy, who gave me a courteous bow and handed me a package with a letter. It said, wait now, I don't know if I remember the words... wait, yes yes, now I got it:

> *These few simple words of mine,*
> *written with tears and dried with sighs,*
> *Be they given to Heaven in the hand of the Sun.*

Antonia — Oh for God's sake.

Nanna — Inside was a long ranty eulogy. He told me he'd taken my hair which had been shorn off in church and made a necklace of it, then he went on about how my brow was more serene than heaven, and saying my lashes were like ebony and my cheeks like milk and cream; my teeth he compared to strings of pearls, my lips to apple blossoms, and made a great thing of my hands, even praising my fingernails. My voice like a rendition of *Gloria in Excelsis,* and coming to my tits he burst into rapture, saying they were like two pert little apples, fresh as snow. Then he came to the fountain of my sex, saying he'd been unworthy to drink from it, saying my juices were like a manna from heaven and my pubes like silk. He didn't say anything about my dirty pepper, saying they'd need to resurrect the poet Barchiello in order to do justice to the least of its wonders. He finished up by thanking me *per infinita saecula* for the liberality with which I'd let him use my treasures, and swearing he would come to see me soon, and with a 'Farewell my darling, my sweetheart', he signed it:

> *He who on your beautiful breast lives,*
>
> *Driven by excess of love, this confession gives.*

Antonia — I'm sure the drawers just fell right off ya.

Nanna — Havin read it, I folded it up and kissed it and put it between my breasts. Then, takin the paper from the package, I saw my lover had sent me a very pretty prayer book. At least that's what I thought. It was covered with green velvet, which signifies love. I turned it over in my hands with a smile and gazed at it lovingly, and praised it as the most beautiful I'd ever seen. Then I dismissed the messenger, tellin him to give his master a kiss for me. Once I was alone I opened the little book to read the *Magnificat,* but saw immediately it was full of paintings of people toyin with themselves the way the nuns had. There was this one picture with a nun stickin her hole through a bottomless basket at the end of the rope, and she was being lowered down onto this monster pepperoni, and I burst out laughin so loudly one of the sisters came runnin. 'What are you laughing at?' she said, and I showed her the booklet and we had a right hoot, but we also got so curious that we wanted to try out the positions, which meant we were forced to employ the glass happy-stick. My companion nestled it so neatly between her thighs that she seemed just like a man with his prick stood high, so I lay down on my back and put my legs on her shoulders, and she took turns pokin me with it, first in the saintly way and then in the devilish way, and Christ, she made me come quickly. Then we switched and she got on her back, and we swapped her pudding for my cake.

Antonia — Do you know what happens to me Nanna when I hear you talk?

Nanna — What?

Antonia — It's like I've been given something to sniff, and now my plumbing is all on the rage.

Nanna — Ha ha ha!

Antonia — Your stories are so lifelike that you get me a bit moist, and I haven't even touched the wine.

Nanna — Now who's talking in riddles? You're talkin like you're tellin stories to little girls: 'I have this thing which is white like a goose, but it's not a goose—can you tell me what it is?'

Antonia — Yeah well, see what you've done to me? You have me talkin in circles.

Nanna — Ah, thank you. Well, let's get on with it. After foolin around with each other, we felt like makin an appearance at confession, but we couldn't get to it because all the nuns had swarmed there and the church looked like St. Peter's on the day of the Stations. Even the monks and soldiers were there, and I even saw Jacob the Jew there who was whispering away with the Mother Superior.

Antonia — Aw, this is a corrupt world.

Nanna — True, and whoever wants it can have it. I also saw one of those wretched Turks who'd been caught in Hungary.

Antonia — He should've become a Christian.

Nanna — I couldn't tell if he was there to get baptised or not. But I've been a fool to tell you I could relate the life of nuns to you in a single day, for what they manage to squeeze into a single hour it would take me a year to narrate. The sun's setting, so I'll wrap things up.

Antonia — Let me say somethin. You told me at the start that this world is no longer what it was in your day; I thought you were gonna tell stories about nuns in the old days, like the stories in the books of the Holy Fathers.

Nanna — I think you heard me wrong; what I meant to say was that nuns are no longer like what they were in the old days.

Antonia — So your tongue slipped.

Nanna — Eh, whatever. I can't even remember what I said. Before we finish, let's get to the most important thing. I should say that, I was tempted by the Devil, and I was lettin this friar fresh from the university put the mickey to me, but I still had an eye for the Bachelor. This friar often took me to dinner outside the convent, not knowin I was wed to the Bachelor. He came for me one evenin after the *Ave Maria* and said: 'My little angel, I want to take you to this place where you'll have a great time—we'll not only listen to angelic music, but we'll see a very good comedy too.' And because I was a bit of an airhead, I got undressed immediately and put on my boy's clothes, which my first lover had made for me. I put a green silk hat on my head and threw on a cloak, then we left. Not far out of the convent we turned up a tiny alleyway and reached a dead end. He gave a whistle, and right away we heard someone come down the stairs. A door opened and we were led up a staircase to a very sumptuous salon. The pageboy who'd led us there said, 'Enter your lordships!', and we went in. No sooner were we inside than everyone got to their feet with their caps in hand, like the congregation does when the preacher announces the blessing. The place was a refuge for religious couples, full of more nuns and monks than there are witches on a full moon. When everyone had sat down again, all I heard were people whispering about my pretty face... I don't like to say it, you know, but I really was very pretty.

Antonia — Hey, you're a beautiful old woman. You must have been a stunning young girl.

Nanna — While I was being flattered so, the music started, music that moved my very soul. There were four singers and one on the lute, singing a song of divine eyes so pure, and after this came a woman from Ferrara whose dance made everyone marvel. You shoulda seen her spinning around in a pirouette with her left leg up like a crane's, her petticoat swirling so fast you could barely make it out.

Antonia — God bless her.

Nanna — Ha ha ha! I'm laughin at another fella, who they called the son of Ciampolo, a Venetian I think, who hid behind a door and imitated a whole host of voices. First of all he aped a porter, and there wasn't a man in there wasn't fooled by it; the porter asked an old woman for the lady of the house, and in the voice of the old woman replied: 'And what do you want of the lady?' He said, in such a pained voice, 'O lady, I'm dying here, I feel like my lungs are boiling—if you'd only give me a glass of water.' He entreated the old woman in a very sweet voice, then he began to fondle her, laughin and sayin things to make her break her Lenten fast. Her senile old husband showed up and raised a roar at the porter as if there was a villain plucking at his cherry tree, and the porter merely laughed and taunted him. 'Drop dead!' the old man cried. 'Drunkard! Fool!' Later when the old man had fallen asleep and the wife had tucked him in, the porter returned and laughed and cried so much with the lady of the house that she let him tickle her muff.

Antonia — Ha ha!

Nanna — You would've laughed at the noises of their fumbling as well as all the porter's sly remarks, and all his cries of 'Lady, do it to me!' Anyway, after all that was over we retired to an alcove where all those who were to act in the comedy were gathered. The curtain was just about to be raised when someone started beatin on the door outside. The curtain went up at the same time the door opened, and there was the Bachelor. He'd just happened along by chance, no idea that I was betraying him. He came in anyhow and saw me there in the lap of the student, and driven by that same murderous passion that drove the mastiff to kill the bitch—it blinds them all—he took me by the hair and dragged me through the hall and down the stairs, ignoring the pleading of everyone on my behalf. Except for the student, who after seeing the Bachelor, disappeared in a flash. The Bachelor kicked my arse all the way back to the convent, and in front of all the nuns gave me a right whipping, as if I was a friar caught fartin during mass. He took the skin clean off my arse with his flogging, but what hurt most of all was that the Mother Superior didn't have my back. After eight days of oils and rose water, I sent word to my mother that if she wanted to see me alive again she'd need to come and get me right away. She hardly recognised me, thinkin I'd been ravaged by fasting and abstinence and morning masses. She insisted I come home at once. And not the begging of all those friars and nuns could make me stay there a day longer. At home, my daddy who feared my mother more than God himself, wanted to send for the doctor, but my mother wouldn't let him because she was afraid of the gossip. And since I couldn't hide the wounds on my arse, I told them that in order to mortify my flesh I'd sat on the stove... my mother was havin none of it, but she kept quiet.

Antonia — You know what, I'm startin to think it might be more trouble than it's worth, makin Pippa a nun. Now I remember that my mother used to tell all sorts of stories about this certain nun who used to feign all kinds of illnesses just so the doctor would come and give her the full treatment.

Nanna — I know exactly who you're talkin about, but I left her out of it so I wouldn't be goin on all day. Since I've kept you here for hours, I want you to come to mine this evenin.

Antonia — As you please.

Nanna — You can help me take care of a few little things, then tomorrow after breakfast, right here in the vineyard, we'll begin the tale of the life of a married woman.

Antonia — I'm all yours.

The two women set out for Nanna's house on the Via della Scrofa where they arrived at dusk. Pippa gave Antonia lots of hugs, and when the time for supper came around they dined, sat about for a bit, then went to bed.

Here ends the first day
of the whimsical Dialogues of Aretino.

HERE BEGINS

the second day of the whimsical Dialogues of Pietro Aretino,
in which Nanna tells Antonia of the life of Wives.

Nanna and Antonia arose at precisely the hour the daft old cuckold Titonus was getting up to try and hide his Lady Aurora's petticoats so she wouldn't venture out to her daylight shenanigans, but catching on to him she snatched her clothes from the auld curmudgeon and left him there whingeing, and went off painted and powdered determined to get the leg over at least a dozen times just to wind up the silly fool.

When the two women had dressed and before the clock struck, Antonia took care of all those chores that plagued poor Nanna more than troubled St. Peter in his ramshackle hut. Once they'd filled their bellies, they returned to the vineyard and sat down under the same fig tree as the day before, and since the hour had come when one chases the day's heat with the fan of idle chatter, Antonia rested her palms on her knees, turned to Nanna and said:

Right, so now I'm clear about the nuns. I swear, after I lay down last night I wasn't able to shut my eyes, thinkin about all the deluded mothers and daft fathers who think that just cause their daughter becomes a nun and doesn't get married, that the desire in her is extinguished—poor creatures! They should know these are flesh-and-blood girls, and that there's nothin increases desire for a thing more than forbidding it. Speakin for myself, I die of thirst if there isn't a drop of wine in the house. And you know, there might be some truth in the proverbs; you know the one that says nuns are the wives of the holy—in fact, the wives of everyone. I'd forgotten about that yesterday, or I wouldn't have given you such a hard time when you were tellin me about all their foolin around.

Nanna — Ach, it's all for the best.

Antonia —Nanna, your door is always open to me, and nothing exceeds your generosity. Thank God I asked you what the matter was yesterday—your stories were a blessing. I'm thrilled you told me everything you did. But I've been twistin and turnin ever since I woke up this mornin—that's why I had to come back today. So tell me, after you took the whipping that turned you sour on love and the convent, what'd your auld girl do?

Nanna — Put it about she wanted to marry me off, is what she did. She came up with one story after another about why I'd been de-nunned. Told everyone there were more devils in the monastery than there are honey biscuits in Siena. So when all this came to the ear of this certain old man, he decided he'd take me as his wife, and because he was well off, my mammy—who wore the pants in our house, like I already said—decided I was gonna marry him. That's how it all happened. To cut to the chase, the night came when he was supposed to 'take my cherry'. The old fella was lyin in the marital bed like a ploughman a-waitin the untilled earth. But my mother knew my virginity had long been robbed, so she came up with a cunning solution. She slaughtered one of the capons that were a gift for the wedding and filled an eggshell with its blood. And after instructin me how to appear chaste and pure and how I was to lie down in the bed, she smeared the blood all over my gash. So when I went to bed and the old man slithered up on me, he found me all tensed up in a knot on the edge of the bed. When he tried to put his hand on my hoo-haa, I threw myself down on the floor, and he leapt off the bed to help me up. 'I don't want to do those bad things, let me alone,' I said, shoutin. My mother heard us and burst in through the door with a lamp in hand. And she gave me a cuddle and told me it was alright, and told me the right thing to do was let the old man stick me with his shepherd's whistle, and he all the while was tryin so hard to prise open my thighs he was sweatin like a glassblower's arse. By this time he'd ripped my nightgown and was cursin me up and down. I've seen more composure from one of those wailin lunatics they tie to the column in the church to try and drive out the Devil. Finally he convinced me to let him stick it in me, so he climbed up on top of me all shakin and sweaty and tried to bury his axe in my axe-wound, but just then I gave such a jolt that I bucked him off. He climbed patiently back in the saddle and went at me again with the haft, and gave it such a shove that he jammed it right in me. Getting the taste of baguette again after all that time, I let go and let him have at me, and didn't cry out until the bishop slipped out of the rectory. Then I began to shriek so loudly the neighbours bolted outside to see what was goin on; my mother rushed back inside too. And when they saw the blood that was all over the bed and his nightshirt, my mother kicked up such a fuss that he let me go and spend the night with her. In the mornin the whole neighbourhood was gathered about discussing my purity, intact until the night before, and when the honeymoon came to an end, I started to attend all the masses and the festivals just like all the other married women. Soon I became intimate with some of them.

Antonia — I got lost for a moment there. Go on.

Nanna — I became friends with a rich and beautiful woman, the wife of a very successful merchant. She was so young and pretty and he was so in love with her, so much he'd spend all night dreamin how he could make her happy in the mornin. One day I was alone with her in her bedroom, and my eyes fell upon the closet. I thought I saw something movin inside.

Antonia — Oh?

Nanna — I kept my eye turned to it. It was, I couldn't quite make it out...

Antonia — Uh-huh...

Nanna — The friend noticed where I was lookin, and I noticed her noticing me, and lookin straight at her, I said: 'When does your husband get back?' 'God knows,' she replied, 'but if it was up to me, then never.' 'Oh? Why?' I asked. 'A plague and a bad Easter may God strike down upon whoever first mentioned him to me. I swear on the crucifix, he's not what others think he is.' She made a quick sign of the cross with her hand and kissed it. 'But why not?' I said. 'You're the envy of every woman in town. Why does he make you unhappy, tell me please.' And she said: 'You want me to spell it out for you? Sure, he looks good out on the piazza, but all his promises are nothing but smoke and air. People need something else. The Bible itself says—man does not live on bread alone.' Whatever she was sayin, she was really tryin to sell it to me. So I said: 'You are very wise, and you know good things come to those who wait.' 'So you can be even more certain of my wisdom,' she said, 'let me show you how a smart woman lives.' She led me to the closet and opened it, and fed my hand inside, and I seemed to put the hand to somethin that was more meat than bread. And right then, without a pause, she pulled a fellow from the closet and laid him down on the bed, climbin up on him and slippin her sleeve over his meat mallet and ridin him until he put his dripping inside her. Then she turned to me and said, 'I'd rather you know me as an unhappy woman who's content than one who's good and desperate.'

Antonia — Those words should be carved in gold.

Nanna — Then she called her maid, her confidante, and had the man sent out the back, but not before adorning him with the chain she wore around her neck. I kissed her on the forehead, the mouth and both cheeks then hurried home before my husband returned because I wanted to see if our manservant was cut from the same cloth. I went in and banished my maid upstairs, then went to my husband's little workroom, walkin quietly, pretendin I'd only come down to use the toilet. I heard whispering, put my ear to the door and listened for a while. It was my mother. She'd already conceived of the same matter and had beaten me to it. So I gave her my blessing, turned around and went back upstairs, dyin of desire because of what I'd seen at my friend's house. The waster of a husband was back in a jiffy so I worked off my horn on him. Not what I was hopin for, but hey...

Antonia — What were you hopin for?

Nanna — Anything is better than your own husband—just think about the pleasure you get from dining out, for example.

Antonia — Aye. It takes a variety of sweetmeats to truly whet the appetite. And I believe you, because men also say that anything is better than the wife.

Nanna — Now, it happened that one time I went out to our country house, where I made the acquaintance of a great lady. I'll call her 'great' and let's leave it at that. Anyway, this woman was drivin her husband nuts cause she wanted to stay in the country all year round, and whenever he'd gush about the city and whine about the countryside, she'd say, 'I don't care about comforts. I don't want to make people green with envy, I don't rate parties or festivals and I don't want to break my neck trying to keep up appearances. Sunday mass is enough for me, and don't get me started on the savings we make by staying here and not throwing lavish parties in the city. So go if you wish, but I'm staying.' The gentleman couldn't help it, he couldn't stay away even if he wanted to. So he left her be in the countryside, sometimes for as much as two whole weeks.

Antonia — I think I know what was on her mind...

Nanna — The priest was on her mind, the chaplain of the parish. I'm tellin ya, if the priest's income had been as big as the sprinkler with which he lashed her ladyship with holy oil, he'd have lived better than a monsignor. Oh, he'd a big ol' third arm. It was a monster.

Antonia — Oh, you devil.

Nanna — How it came about was, one day *our-lady-of-the-country* caught sight of the priest takin a piss behind a tree right below her window—it was she herself told me all this, she gave me the whole story. Anyway, she saw this foot-long *melanzano melanzano* with a shiny red tip cleft to perfection, and with a big swollen vein runnin up the shaft. It wasn't quite hard and neither was it flaccid, but had a glorious curve on it shaped like an aubergine just so, nestled nicely in golden blond hair, and below it, two heavy, firm round plums, lovelier than the eggs that the eagle tucked in its nest sits lovingly on. Soon as she saw those tremendous jewels, she threw herself on the floor for fear of shoutin at him to come up.

Antonia — You know how they say if a woman's pregnant and touches her nose while she's lookin at something incredible, it'll manifest in her child. Well, imagine she'd touched her nose while lookin at the priest and the child was born with the birthmark of those balls on its face.

Nanna — Ha ha ha! Anyway, after throwin herself on the floor she came over in such a frenzy for his fleshy flute she dead fainted and had to be carried to the bed. Her husband, perplexed at the affair, sent for the doctor who came and took her pulse and asked her why she was so damp between the thighs.

Antonia — I swear, these doctors don't know what to say when they come across a woman who has healthy plumbing down there.

Nanna — Aye, you're right. The doctor had ideas about prescribing a certain stiff cure, but when she roundly rejected him it brought tears to her husband's eyes to hear her call for the priest. 'I want to confess,' she said, 'and if it pleases God that I die, it will please me too. I will be sad to leave you, my dear husband.' When he heard these words, the husband threw himself around her neck weeping. 'Courage,' she said, givin him a kiss. Then she gave such a squeal it was as if she was givin up the ghost. The husband called for the priest again. A servant was sent and the priest came in a state of confusion. As he arrived, the doctor, still at her side, took her pulse and was stumped that it seemed to beat faster. The priest appeared before her and said: 'May God restore your health.' As he stepped close, she couldn't take her eyes off his hefty codpiece, which bulged under the priest's rough woollen blouse. She fainted again from anguish. After they'd bathed her wrists in rosewater, she somewhat revived. Then the husband, who was a world-class eejit, cleared the room and closed the door, so that they might not listen in on her confession. He deliberated with the doctor, spewin all kinds of nonsense. And while the two of them prestidigitated, the priest sat down on the side of the bed and made the sign of the cross so she wouldn't have to raise her head. He was just about to ask how long it had been since her last confession, when she grabbed at his bell-rope, which instantly lifted its head to the heavens.

Antonia — Whadda girl!

Nanna — Eh! And what do you think about this priest, who dispelled her dizziness with a couple of quick blessings?

Antonia — I say he deserves praise for not being one of these chickenshits who pisses the bed then shouts, 'Look how much I've sweated!'

Nanna — Once the confession was over the priest sat next to her and placed his hand on her forehead. The husband put his head around the door right then, and seein her receiving the absolution, came over. Findin her all brightened in the face, he said: 'There's no better physician than the Lord God Almighty. You look completely restored, and only an hour ago I thought I was certain to lose you.' She turned to him and sighed: 'I am reborn.' Muttering with her confessor, her hands clasped in prayer, she pretended to say penance. When the priest was dismissed, she made the husband put a ducat and two julios in his hand, sayin: 'The julios are alms for the confession, and the ducat so you can say a few masses for St. Gregory.'

Antonia — Add that to the others!

Nanna — Wait til I tell you a story even wilder than the priest's tale. There was a forty-year-old lady in our village who was very rich, came from a very noble family and was the wife of a doctor, a man who'd accomplished miracles with his learnings and with which he'd filled many great books. This lady, I'm tellin you, went about dressed in a monk's brown robe. If in a day she'd not heard five or six masses, she'd be laid out in mortal agony for the rest of it. She had more prayers on her than a rosary; she was a proper saint-raver, a Bible-basher, fasted on every Friday of the month and not just in March, and she responded to every prayer of the mass like a choirboy and sang the hymns like a monk. They even say she had a chastity belt on her.

Antonia — Aye right. I piss on all the saints.

Nanna — Hey, this woman did a hundred more penances than all the saints combined. She wore only wooden clogs, and on the eve of St. Francis and the feast of the Ascension, she ate only as much bread as you can hold in your fist and drank a single sip of water, prayed til midnight, and slept—for all she slept—on a bed of nettles.

Antonia — Without a nightgown?

Nanna — I've no idea. Now, there was this hermit, a right holy-joe, lived in a hermitage a mile from this lady's manor, and every day he came through the village for a few scraps to eat. He never went home empty-handed, because the sack that covered him, his haggard face, the beard that hung down to his belt, and the weird stone he held in his hand like St. Jerome, filled the whole village with pity. It was this hermit the charity of the doctor's wife alighted on. Her husband, of course, stayed in the city. She often visited the hermitage, which was a den of devoutness, and she'd leave here carryin a handful of bitter salads, because she felt it too immoral to eat the sweet ones.

Antonia — Where was the hermitage?

Nanna — On top of a very steep hill. It was called Calvary. In the middle of it was a huge wooden crucifix with three iron nails, around its neck a crown of thorns and over the crossbar hung a whip of braided cord, and at its foot the skull of a dead man. To the side of it a spear stuck out of the ground with a pierced sponge atop it, and on the other side a rusty halberd. All of which scared the bejaysus outta the peasant women. The hermitage had a garden enclosed by a wall of reeds which had a gate made of willow. You could've dug around in the garden all day and wouldn't have upturned a single stone. The plots were full of herbs: wild thyme, mint, aniseed, sweet marjoram, parsley... and all kinds of greens besides. And right in the centre, a great big almond tree covered the whole place in shade. Out of the living stones of the hill bubbled a spring which cascaded through the garden, and anytime the hermit could escape from his prayers, he'd tend to the garden. Not far from it stood a little church with a bell tower. This hermit's hut was built against the wall of this church. So, into this little paradise arrived the doctor's wife, and in order not to give the body cause to envy the spirit, one day they withdrew to his small hut in order to escape the sun's torture. I don't know how it came about, but it ended in the sins of the flesh. And while they were makin the beast with two backs, a peasant out lookin for his donkey passed the hut by chance and spied the holy couple in the Devil's disarray. He ran straight to the village and rang the bell, callin out the people, who, upon hearin the news, quit work and convened in the church. The peasant was there relating to the priest how the hermit was performing miracles of a sort. So the priest vested himself in the holy garb, stole around his neck and holy book in hand, and with the clerk out ahead of him brandishing the cross, and fifty comin behind, soldiered out to the hut in less a time than it takes to recite a *credo*. There they found the handmaiden of the heavens and God's abstinent exhausted and asleep arm in arm. And would you believe it, the hermit was snorin away, with his langer still stuck in her brown bell. Castin eyes upon em, the crowd fell silent. But seein their wives turn away, the men began to laugh and this woke the couple up. The priest, seein how they were stuck together faster than a joint, cried over the roarin of the crowd: '*Et incarnatus est!*'

Antonia — I thought no one could outdo the nuns for whorin. I was wrong. But tell me, were the hermit and the hypocrite put to death?

Nanna — Put to death? Once he'd slipped his tool out of her dirty toolbox, the hermit rose to his feet and gave himself two lashes of the whip he wore around his waist. Then he said: 'Gentlemen, read the lives of the Holy Fathers, and then, by fire, judge me how you see fit. It was the Devil usurped my being and sinned in my stead. It would be a grave error to hurt him.' Now wait til I tell you... This old lecher, who'd first been a soldier then a murderer, a ruffian too, and to escape his past had made himself a hermit, he began to run his mouth off and wouldn't stop, and was so convincing that everyone—except me, who knew well where the Devil hid his tail—even the priest, took him at his word about the demons who'd taken control of him. While the besacked hermit was bullshittin em all, this nun in masquerade had time to come up with her own deception, and began to writhe on the floor, grippin her throat with two hands and chokin herself, eyes poppin from her head, and she screamed in such torment she struck terror into the hearts of the villagers. Then the hermit turned and said: 'Behold the evil spirit that has possessed this woman.' When the mayor of the village tried to restrain her, she bit him and shrieked. She was at last bound up by ten peasants and carried to the church, where they touched her with two little bones which they said were the Bones of the Innocents, which were kept as relics in the tabernacle. After they'd touched her a third time she came to her senses. Word was sent to the doctor, who took our little saint back to the city and had a sermon said in her name.

Antonia — That is the most sleeked thing I've ever heard.

Nanna — Believe me, I could tell you much worse.

Antonia — I'm not so sure...

Nanna — Mother of God, yes. There was a neighbour of mine in the countryside, a real beauty, the prettiest bird on the perch. They all had eyes for her. All night long you heard nothin but serenades, and all through the day men prancin by on their horses. When she was on her way to mass so many of em gathered they'd block the street, crossin themselves and appealin to Holy Mary. 'Blessed'll be he who enjoys such an angel', one would say, and another: 'Lord my God, let me kiss her tit and I'll die happy'. Some men gathered up the dirt she stepped on and dusted their caps with it like holy incense. Others looked at her and simply sighed and said not a word. This fabled sea, where many men fished but landed nary a catch. But one day onto this sea came a real sleazebag, one of these wandering pedagogues that go house to house spreadin their cankerous message. He was the greasiest, the most wretched, degenerate filthbag you've ever laid eyes on. His neck was so greasy the lice'd slide right off him. Ragged he was.

Antonia — I can picture him clearly. A mangey slob.

Nanna — Exactly. Yet somehow he drew the lusty devil out of that lovely girl. To be honest, we women, when we choose, we always choose the worst. So havin taken an eye for him, one night she began feedin her husband a tale of woe a mile long: 'Dear, we're blessed by God and very rich, but we don't have any children and we're unlikely to. So I thought of a great act of mercy.' The good husband says to her: 'What is it, sweetheart?' She says: 'Your sister's coming down with sons and daughters. Why don't we raise her youngest? It'll do our souls good, and after all, charity begins at home, doesn't it?' The husband praised his wife. 'For such a long time I've wanted to ask you this, but I didn't think you'd want to. But now I know how you really feel, I'll go first thing tomorrow and give her the good news, and bring the boy right here.' And so it went. With the gratitude of his sister, the husband went and brought back his little nephew, and the wife made a great fuss about the child. A few days later they were sittin at the table, and after dinner she says to him: 'We really must teach our little Luigi some virtue', to which he answered: 'And who do you have in mind?' 'That schoolmaster who's always wandering about town. He must be looking for a position.' 'What schoolmaster?' says he to her. 'The one who wears that filthy robe that's always falling off his back?' 'Yes, that's the one. I can't remember who said it, but they say he's as smart as an encyclopaedia.' 'He might be just the man,' replied the husband, and that same evenin he went out and brought the rooster back to the henhouse, and set him up in the room the mistress readied for him.

Antonia — What was all this dirty scheming about then?

Nanna — Just listen. The very next evenin the woman, holdin her nephew's hand—for the boy's education was to be her cover—called the pedagogue and said (and I heard it, for I was dinin there that night), 'Master, more than this boy here, it is me you will have to teach.' And sayin this she kissed him right on the mouth. 'And in regards to your payment, leave it to me.' The schoolmaster answered by rattlin off a whole schpeel in church Latin, puttin forward his argument with a whole series of points and counterpoints, at which the lady of the house turned to me and said: 'He's a regular Cicero!' They went on talkin in this pig-Latin, until she eventually blurted out: 'Tell me, master, were you ever in love?' The arsewipe, whose tail was thicker than a peacock's, replied: 'M'lady, twas love that drove me to my studies.' At this he churned out the whole history, tellin us about this one who'd hanged herself because of him, and one who'd drank poison, another who'd thrown herself from a tower, and even had the gall to recite a list of names he said were the women who'd gone straight to hell because of him. And he did it all with a very fine elocution. And while he was yabberin on, she kept nudgin me and whisperin, 'What do you think of the master?' I saw the cut of him and I knew the sort he was, I said, 'He's so good at shakin the peach tree he might even bring down a pear.' She howled and threw her arms around my neck, and sendin him off to study she took me to her bedroom. Then came a message from her husband that he wouldn't make it home that night, as sometimes happened, and happy about this, she said to me: 'Your old dodderer will have to be left alone too, because this evening I want you to stay with me.' I sent word to my mother and got permission to stay. We treated ourselves to a right feast: liver, sweetbreads, chickens' feet, salad and a whole capon, olives, apples and cheeses, and quince to settle our stomachs, and candies to sweeten our breath. A dinner of hard-boiled eggs was sent to the Master in his room—and you can probably imagine why.

Antonia — It hit me right away.

Nanna — After we'd finished and the table had been cleared, and the nephew had been sent to bed, she says to me: 'Sister, if our husbands eat whatever meat they like whenever they want, why then tonight shouldn't we enjoy the Master's flesh? Judging by the size of his nose he must have a prick like an emperor's. And anyway, no one will ever know. He's so ugly and clumsy, even if he told anyone they'd never believe him.' I pretended to be afraid, and flinched. 'This is dangerous talk, sister—if your husband comes home, imagine what would happen to us.' 'Are you daft? Don't you think if my husband came back I'd know how to handle him?' And I says to her: 'If that's the case, then go right ahead.' Well, the crafty schoolmaster had noticed how worked up the lady got when she talked to him about love, and well aware the man of the house was away, had snuck up to the door and put his ear to it, listenin to everything was said. And the lady, havin listened to the stories about all those daft eejits who'd hung themselves or strangled themselves on his account, decided the best course of action would be to let him give her a good stuffing and be done with it. Well, the master had heard the lot, and stuck-up as he was, threw open the door and walked in without invitation. As soon as she saw him, his mistress cried: 'Maestro, put a cork in your mouth—tonight, I have only use for your big rule-stick.' The clumsy dog, who hadn't a nose for roses nor fingers to stop a flute, couldn't have given a rat's for foreplay; he just unleashed his baby's leg all covered with lumps and with a big inflamed head, gave it a proud slap and said, 'I am at my lady's pleasure.' Takin him in hand, she said: 'Oh my sparrow, my dove, my pigeon, come into the palace of my aviary!' Backin up against the wall, she lifted a leg and thrust it right up inside her, and stood there as he poked away at her rough as ya like. What'd I do? Well, there's no point gettin jealous while others have all the pleasure. I sat back in the chair and took a pestle—which must have been used for poundin cinnamon from the smell of it—and gave myself a good little diddling. The goat didn't take long emptyin his sack, and the lady, ragged but still with the horn on her, sat down on the little bed and again took the dog by the tail, and tugged and twisted it so much that it grew all red and hoary again, and since she was revolted by the teacher's face, turned herself around, grabbed the schoolmaster's *salvum me fac* and drove it furiously into her squeeze box, then pulled it out and rammed it in again, and then again into her truffle tunnel, and when the second round ended they collapsed in a heap. Then she turns to me and says: 'There's plenty of this big pepperoni left if you want some.' I felt a bit turned, and even though I was hot for it I was like someone starving but couldn't eat. I was content to flick the bean—that little secret the Bachelor had taught me about—but we were disturbed when we heard this pounding on the door downstairs. At this the schoolmaster took on the look of a man who's been rumbled breakin into the sacristy, and the two of us, faces frozen, didn't move. When she recognised her husband's cries, and was sure he'd heard what had been goin on upstairs, she shouted down: 'Who's out there?' 'It's me!' he wailed. 'Oh dear—I'm coming down, wait right there!' She turned to us: 'Nobody move,' and with that, went out and down the stairs and opened to the man of the house. 'My love,' she said, 'a spirit told me: "Don't go to bed, because it's certain your husband will return tonight", and so I didn't fall asleep. I asked our neighbour to stay with me. The poor thing, she's been telling me all about the life she had in the convent, and it has me terribly upset. And if I hadn't asked our schoolmaster to come and cheer me up with his nonsense, I would've had a terrible night.' Then, without another word, she led him upstairs, and he laughed himself silly when he saw the schoolmaster, who'd a face on him like the spirit had been slapped from his soul. But when the husband looked at me, he got to plottin how he might take possession of my little purse, and in order to ingratiate himself with me, engaged in tomfoolery with the schoolmaster, gettin him to recite his ABCs backwards, and the scoundrel, making a lark of it, made the husband laugh til he fell over. For my part, I knew a roving eye when I saw one—he was even playin footsy with me. So I said: 'Since the maids have gone off to bed, I'll go and bed down with them.' 'No, no!' he says, turning to his wife. 'Take her to the small room and put her in there.' I was bustled off to the room, and when I was tucked in he said, loudly so I'd hear: 'Dear wife, I must get back to business. Send this joker off to bed and go and lay your own head down.' She was so happy she could've kissed the heavens, and began puttin out her dress for the next day to show how eager she was to see him the followin mornin. The husband, he made a great show of goin down the stairs and bangin the door on his way out, except he went nowhere and stayed hidden inside the house. Then he crept back up the stairs like a cat, into my room where I lay awake, and slipped into the bed next to me. When he put a hand on my tit, the thunder and terror of passion came over me; it felt like when you're lyin in bed at night, half-dreamin, and it's like somethin weighs down upon your chest and you can't move.

Antonia — That's what they call a nightmare.

Nanna — Aye, so it is. Then he whispers to me: 'Best keep quiet,' and he gently stroked my cheek. 'Who is this?' I said. 'It's only me,' replied the night visitor, all the while tryin to prise open my thighs, which were clenched tighter than a miser's fist. Then I cried out: 'O my lady!' and she heard me. The husband, who was all over me, leapt from the bed and ran out the side door, just as his wife came in, lamp in hand, to see what was up. The husband then went into the room she'd just come out of, seein the goat of a schoolmaster in the bed rubbin his big rashy rod, waitin to put songs on the lark. And just as that twisty bitch was sayin to me, 'What's wrong with you?', a braying like that of a donkey put paid to my reply. The husband was in there beatin the schoolmaster with the fire shovel, and if the wife hadn't rushed in and pulled him from his blows, he'd have ended in pieces.

Antonia — He'd good reason to beat seven shades o'shite outta him.

Nanna — He had, and he hadn't.

Antonia — How the hell not?

Nanna — There's a lot could be said about the whole affair. When the wife saw the blood pour from the eejit's face, she rounded on the husband who'd lost all respect for her after findin that dirty dick in his bed. She had a go at him all the same: 'What kinda woman do you take me for, eh? My nurse told me the truth when she said you'd treat me like a street whore, whereas it's I who's lifted you up. Her predictions have all come true, cause she kept telling me, "Don't take him because he'll mistreat you". You think a woman like me would go with a squint-eyed louse like him, huh? Why did you beat him, tell me? What'd you see him do? Is our bed a holy altar that deserves such respect? Well, now I see you for what you are. If that's the way you want to play it, tomorrow morning I'll wrap things up and get the notary to sign my will. That'll show you—what kind of man makes a whore out of his wife without justification?' And she went on, howlin: 'Is that the sort of woman I am, eh?' She tore at her hair so wildly you'd have thought her father had been murdered before her very eyes. By this time I was all dressed and had run in. I said to her: 'Do you want to start the whole neighbourhood gossiping about you? Come on now, quiet.'

Antonia — And what did bully boy say to that?

Nanna — He lost his balls at the threatening with the will, for he knew a man without property is worse off than a pimp without an income.

Antonia — That's not just waffle.

Nanna — I laughed at the schoolmaster in his nightgown, cowering in the corner.

Antonia — He must have looked like a fox in the trap, with the blows rainin down on him.

Nanna — Ha ha! You said it. The husband, who didn't want to give up his cherry tree simply because the donkey had taken a nibble at it, knelt at her feet and begged and pleaded. She forgave him. And I ate the dry bread of repentance, since I stuck to my guns. And after drivin the schoolmaster to bed with a dozen blows of the shovel, they went to bed too, pacified, and I followed. The next mornin my mother showed up and sent me straight home, and I spent the whole day in a daze because of the crazy night I'd spent.

Antonia — Was the schoolmaster run out?

Nanna — Run out? I saw him eight days later, all dressed up to the nines like a gentleman.

Antonia — One thing's for sure, when a servant or a butler is dressin and spendin beyond his means, he's dippin his beak in the mistress.

Nanna — No doubt about it. But let's get to another story. This one is about a certain lady who wanted to have her furrow ploughed by a peasant who was said to be hung like a mule. She was the wife of an aged knight of Pope John, who had more airs about his station than the fella who wipes the Pope's arse. He was always struttin about with his head in the air, and to every address sent his way he'd begin his reply, 'We knights...', as if there was nothin else worth talkin about. When he appeared on the feast days dressed in all his fine attire, his head would fill the whole church, and he'd mince about discussing the great Turk and the Sultan in Latin, and he had a worldly knowledge he never stopped spewin. Now the wife of this pure pest used to whine about everything that was delivered from their country estate, and if it was chickens that came, she'd say: 'What, this is it? We've been robbed!', and if it was fruits, 'What a bunch of crooks these peasants are—they keep the ripe stuff for themselves and give the green ones to us'. If it was greens, or game, or strawberries or suchlike, she'd say, 'We're being stiffed! I don't want these—we're paying through the nose for this stuff in wine and oil'. She kicked up such a fuss she made her husband suspicious, and in the end he fired the farmhand, and, on

his wife's prompting, made a deal with the man with the big pole she'd
an eye on for shakin out her cherry tree. After the lease was signed, the
peasant took over the holding. A few days later he came to the town,
so laden with wares he'd to knock the door with his foot. The door was
opened to him and he went up the stairs. He'd a yoke over his back
that held three pairs of chickens and three of capons, and in his right
hand a basket filled with a hundred eggs and all sorts of cheeses. And
with a wink and a bow, he struck the floor with his boot and presented
the goods to the mistress. The farmhand's reputation goin before
him, she gave him a welcome that would have floored her good knight.
She'd a right good tuck laid out for him on the table, and a great mug
of sweet white wine. Seeing the ruddy face on him that pleased her
well, she said: 'Whenever you bring us good things, I'll make sure you
get the enjoyment of them.' And her husband not being at home, she
shouted to the maid, 'Did you hear me?', at which the maid gathered
up the food and stored away the capons and took away the chickens.
The wife led the farmhand up to the attic, and once they were upstairs
they closed the skylight and she asked to see what kind of tool he kept
for tillin fields, to see if it measured up. The maid swore to me later
that next she heard such an unholy racket from above she thought the
ceiling was gonna come in. Makin out like she'd only taken him aside
to discuss the shortcomings of the previous worker, the mistress had
him plough her crooked twice over, then they came back down the
stairs. Since night was upon them and he didn't want to wait about
for the knight to get back, he asked the lady's leave and returned to
the estate in the country, where he wasted no time recounting his
whole adventure to the parish priest. The lady was still marvelling at
the size of his cucumber, which had stuffed her to bursting, when she
heard a ruckus from outside, folk pelting here and there, and someone
shoutin: 'Attack! Attack!' She went out onto the balcony and saw some
of her relatives brandishing swords in a fury, and some with spears,
and even a few with pruning hooks and skewers. Her face turned to

ash when she saw a mob, among which two fellows were carryin her knight who was all covered in blood. She took a swoon and fell to the floor. The broken knight was carried upstairs and laid on his bed, and they sent a man forth to bring the doctor, while others began to make bandages of men's shirts. Meanwhile, the wife came to and went to her husband who stared at her blankly. She began roarin. But when they brought candles to the bedside, she realised he was dyin. She sat next to him and said: 'Forgive me. Give yourself up to God.' With a weak gesture he gave her his forgiveness, then he gave up the ghost. It was too late when the priest and doctor arrived.

Antonia — But how did he die?

Nanna — Because the cheatin harlot had made that dirty yokel very happy, the knight found out about it and went to defend his honour and was sent to his final resting place with three hearty stab wounds. This set the whole region on fire, and in order to save her neck, she twice made out like she wanted to fling herself from a window, makin sure there was time enough for someone to grab her down. She organised a funeral more solemn than had ever been seen, painting his coat of arms on the church walls and draping his coffin in a very ornate brocade. The coffin was carried by six citizens and everyone turned out for the service, gatherin in the church where the good wife, all dressed in black and with two hundred wailing women at her back, gave such a eulogy for her husband there wasn't a dry eye in the house. After the knight's deeds had been recounted by the priest from the pulpit and the *requiem aeternum* had been sung by more than a thousand priests, monks and friars of every stripe, he was laid in a beautiful tomb inscribed with a timeless epitaph and draped with banners, and above the bier was hung his gilded silver sword and his shield and helmet. I forgot to mention—all the workers from his estates attended the funeral and followed the coffin, even the fellow with the capons and the chickens and the eggs... you know, the one from the unfortunate episode. But why waste any more words on it? With the well-hung peasant, she found a way to dry her tears, and since the knight had married her for love, he'd left her his entire estate in his will, much to the dismay of his relatives.

Antonia — She landed on her feet in the end!

Nanna — Now the tart could sally about the countryside without a care in the world. After sendin her servants away, she found that her yokel's big jolly warbler brought her such comfort and consolation. So against all shame, she decided to make him the knight's successor before her family began pestering her to take another husband. And so that she might take her time about cementing her plans, she put it about she was gonna become a nun, and so all the orders began courtin her. But all that aside, she'd resolved to marry the peasant, givin not a thought to, 'What'll they say about me?' or, 'What dishonour will I bring upon the family?', and this, that and the other. Knowin respectability is the death of pleasure and that repentance is ruin, she sent for a notary before any doubts could waylay her.

Antonia — She could've stayed a widow and still satisfied herself with the yokel's door-knocker all the same.

Nanna — I'll tell you some other time why she didn't stay a widow. We could sit here and talk all day about the lives of widows; I'll say only this—a widow is twenty-carat finer a whore than any nun, wife or woman who works the street corners.

Antonia — How's that?

Nanna — Nuns, wives and whores let themselves get diddled by any old dog; but widows are polished and refined by any number of prayers, discipline, devotions, masses, offices and alms, and by all the seven works of mercy besides.

Antonia — Aren't there any worthy nuns, wives, widows or whores?

Nanna — With these four classes you'd be advised to follow the old adage about coins: 'You're wise to take them on faith'.

Antonia — We're doin alright then. Come on then, back to the widow's wedding.

Nanna — In short, she married him. She couldn't let him out of her sight—even in the fields and the vineyard. She brought him his meals, too. Once their relationship was known, however, she had to flee, since the whole town had it in for her, not just her family. And the yokel, who came from a loutish family, stuck the knife in her brother who'd threatened to poison him. It wasn't long before people were afraid to go out the door.

Antonia — Best to stay away from such folk.

Nanna — As the saying goes: 'God save us from clodhoppers'. But let's talk about somethin merrier. After the misery of that poor knight's death, I'll sweeten things with a tale about this rich, stingy old cretin who had a wife of seventeen with the most alluring hips you ever seen, and with such grace that everything she said seemed full of sweetness. She had very refined gestures, a kind of haughty manner, ways about her that set longing in men's hearts. Give her a lute and she seemed a master of music; put a book in her hand and she turned into a poetess, give her a sword and youd've sworn she was a soldier. To see her dance she was a little deer, singing an angel, and to watch her play... well, I haven't the words. There was a certain burning in her eyes, something that lit a heart on fire. Sharp she was and quick of wit, and spoke with such majesty she made duchesses seem daft. She could dress, too— she'd fashion her own garments that would catch everyone's eye. One day she'd be with the hair curled, another with it parted, and the next day with it plaited or maybe with a little curl hanging down over her eye that made her wink. She'd destroy men with desire and women with envy, and because of her natural manner she knew exactly how to cast a spell over a lover, who'd swoon at the trembling of her rosy breasts. Often she'd hold out a hand and study it, as if she was searching for some defect; the glitter of her rings would match her eyes, dazzling anyone who was lost gazing at the hand which she so artfully turned. She scarcely touched the ground when she walked; to see her move was like she was softly dancing. And when holy water was sprinkled on her head, her bow seemed to say, 'Number me among the angels'. And yet all her beauty and her virtues did not stop her pig-headed father marryin her off to this auld sixty-year-old, or at least that's what he told everyone. He could've been older. This husband of hers was called 'Count' for some kind of tumbledown castle he owned with a turret and two bread ovens, and some claim he said was given him by the Emperor. He opened his estate to all the fops around who liked to play court, and every month they gathered there, and those that gathered to watch the fools joust would deign to show him respect. Sometimes he'd show up dressed in a red velvet robe with golden spangles like the Pope, with his sword in an ancient scabbard by his side. He'd circle on foot followed by twenty footmen armed with crossbows, some his servants and some hired from his estates. He rode an old mare fat on bran, and a thousand pairs of spurs couldn't have shifted her. On these days he kept his wife locked up in the castle, though any other day the old hound would follow her from church to field to feast like a dog on the scent. In the sack he gloated about all the valiant deeds he'd performed as a soldier; describing his battles he'd mouth the *badoom!* of the cannons and leap around the bed like a madman. The poor girl, who wanted nothin more than to joust with all the moors of the night, despaired. Sometimes out of pure spite she'd make him crouch on the floor on all fours with a sash in his mouth for a girdle, climb up on him and beat him with her heels and ride him like a horse. And while puttin up with this dull life, she conceived of an amusing trick.

Antonia — Now this I'd like to hear.

Nanna — She began mumbling nonsense in her sleep at night which made the old man chuckle, but he lost his patience and scolded her when she began flailing about in the bed and gave him a crack in the eye with her fist. She pretended not to know what was goin on, and even went so far as to go sleepwalking, openin windows and chests, and even gettin dressed, and the daft old bugger would chase and shout after her. Once it happened that, followin her out of their chamber, he put his foot down unwittingly at the head of the staircase and went arse over elbow all the way to the bottom, breakin his leg. He roused the whole household and even the neighbours with his cries, so they came and put him back in bed—it'd been better had he not got up in the first place. And she, pretendin to come around at her husband's anguish, heard what she'd done and wept, and cursed herself for her terrible affliction. Then she sent for the doctor to come and set her husband's leg bone.

Antonia — And what was all this fakery about?

Nanna — Why to get him to fall, of course, so that, weak in the bed, he couldn't sneak around after her. Now the jealous old man was beyond miserable, but he was so vain he kept around him ten valets that all slept in one chamber on the ground floor, all young lads, the oldest no more than twenty-four. They were a raggedy bunch who lived mostly on bread and scraps.

Antonia — Why did these rogues hang about then?

Nanna — For the freedom he gave em. And Antonia, sweetheart, this lady had given the band the once over, and now that the old man had his leg in a splint, she took to sleepwalkin again, jumpin clean from the bed in the night while the old man shouted, 'Hey, watch out!' And while he was chokin tryin to call after her, she went out the door and downstairs to the valets, who were all gathered on the floor of the room gamblin with money they'd stolen from their daft old master. 'Evening, boys,' she said, then extinguished the lamp and put her hand to the first fella she found, and immediately went to work. During the three hours she was in there, she had a go at all ten of em. Twice over. Then she went back up the stairs well relieved of the horn, and said to her old fool: 'Dear husband, if you're feeling sore about anything, then forgive this evil nature of mine that causes me to drag myself about the house all night like a witch.'

Antonia — Who told you this story in such minute detail?

Nanna — She did. For after havin trod all over her honour, she became the wife of the people. Once her charms became common knowledge she'd tell her stories to any comer, even those who didn't want to hear. What's more, one of the valets got pissed at her because she paid more attention to one of the fellows with a bigger, thicker tool than he had, so he was runnin around tellin the story in every square, tavern and store.

Antonia — So much the worse for the old fool. He should've taken a wife his own age, not one who could've been his daughter a hundred times over.

Nanna — That's an old fool for ya. And it wasn't enough she had the old codger wrapped clean around her pretty finger, but she took a shine to an itinerant busker and decided to douse the old fart's soup with a dose of something, and while he was on the deathbed she married the singer and give him a ride right there in front of the dyin old codger, though I can't swear to this, though, as I didn't hear it firsthand.

Antonia — It's probably true n'all.

Nanna — Now listen to this. One of the better ladies of the city had a husband who was more fond of gambling than a monkey is for bananas, and his favourite game was *primero*. They came to his house in droves to play cards, and because he had an estate close by, a worker of his who'd been widowed would come every fortnight to visit his wife and bring her little treats such as dried figs, walnuts, olives, sultanas and so on. After spendin a few hours in her company, she'd go on her way. One feast day she came to see her mistress and brought a basket of goodies with her, but the weather kicked up while she was there. Terrible wind and rain howled, so she was forced to spend the night. Anyway, this pure dosser of a husband who lived a life of leisure and would say any old thing in front of his wife that came into his head, well, this drunken halfwit got wind of the widow and took a shine to her. And not only that, but he thought he'd make a champion of himself in front of his gambling friends and told them he'd make them a 'thirty-one', and they all laughed and egged him on. He told em to come back after dinner, then said to his wife: 'Put the peasant woman in the attic tonight.' She told him she would and they all sat down to dinner together, the wife puttin the widow, who looked pretty as a picture, at the foot of the table. After dinner the rogues all came back and the husband went off with them, tellin the wife to get to bed and send the peasant woman to her room. The wife, who knew well of his rovin eye, said to herself: 'I've heard that a woman who enjoys it fully once is never again wanting. My shameless husband wants to put siege to her castle and loot her treasury—I'm gonna find out what this "thirty-one" business is that these feckless numpties are preparing for the good woman.' Havin set her mind to it, she put the peasant woman in her own room and lay down to bed in the attic. So along comes her husband, his feet trampin up the stairs, huffin and puffin and moanin like an old dog, and his friends behind him like children—who fully intend to get their fingers in the dough when he's through—when there's a hiccup and all of them start gigglin *'Tee-hee!'*, tryin to conceal the noise. Now the husband slips in next to her with a sigh—and truthfully, she'd never waited for him with so much desire as she did right then—he takes hold of her, his hands seemin to say, 'There's no escaping me now...' She pretends she's woken up in great fear and is tryin to escape, but he grips her tight and pulls her to him, forcin her legs open with his knee. I dunno, but surely when he was balls deep in her you'd think he'd know it was his wife, sure as we can see the leaves on this fig tree above our heads right now. Anyway, feelin him shake her plum tree not like a husband but a lover, she says to herself, 'This dog goes like a hound at another's loaf, while he hardly even touches the bread from his own oven.' He has the ride of her then goes out to his companions, laughin loudly. 'Ooh-wee! Maybe it's the quiet life or just good eatin, but that is one fleshy soft woman. Her ass tasted like mint and wild thyme!' Then he pushes forward the next man, who goes at her like a monk at his beef stew. And when he's done the third man, who creeps up on her and dips his pike in the reservoir, and makes the others crease with laughter by fartin like a trumpet, so that the woman says to herself: 'These degenerates have no discretion.' Anyway, not to keep you here all night rattlin off this fellow and that one, to put it in the way of the Petrarchan whore, Mamma-Don't-Wan'-It, they went at her from every angle, in every way, shape and slant possible. Well, after the twentieth had mounted her she was howlin like a cat from pain and pleasure both. Then came a man who, when it was time to dip his bagpipe, found her cream pie swimmin and decided to take a shot at her chocolate chute, and not findin any hole cried out: 'Woman, hold your nose and take a sniff of my caper.' Upon hearin this the others had the beef whistles on them stand up somethin wicked, and were at the ready waitin to pounce on her like the old women waitin in line for confession during Holy Week. While they were standin there, there was more than one man who beat the bishop and made him spit. And the last four of the team who were mad for it by this stage, but didn't really want to be swimmin around in the muck without a sheath, took the lighted candle and bathed their tackles in wax, and went on in to the room candle in hand. And the wife, now discovered, assumed the brazen expression of a Sisto Bridge whore and said: 'Since I heard it said that this and that woman here had taken the "thirty-one", well, I wanted to find out what all the fuss was about.' Now the husband came in. 'Well, and how did you find it dear wife?' She nodded. 'Not bad. Not bad at all.' And no longer bein able to hold back the flood, she ran to the toilet, unclenched her love muscle, and like a swollen abbot discharges too much soup from his belly, gave twenty-seven unborn souls back to the earthly limbo. The peasant woman, when she heard that the carriage train that was en route to her had pulled into another station, she went home as if her arse had been scalded, and gave her mistress the cold shoulder for a full year.

Antonia — Blessed are those who know how to sate their desires.

Nanna — You said it. But I don't envy anyone who satisfies them with these 'thirty-ones'... I've tried it myself, and I didn't find the joy in them that some do. Christ, I thought it would never end. I'm tellin ya, if it lasted half as long it'd be a fine thing and would be worth the time. But anyway, movin on… let's get to the woman who took a shine to a crook the mayor refused to hang, so as not to give the satisfaction to the gallows. When he was only twenty-one, this prisoner's father had died and left him about 14,000 ducats, half in cash and the rest in possessions. In under three years he'd eaten, gambled and screwed away the whole lot, then he liquidated his father's estates and made short work of it too. Unable to sell the cottage—the will forbade it—he took it down brick by brick and sold the stones. All the furniture went next: beds, sheets, tablecloths, one day this thing, the next somethin else, until there was nothin left and he was left naked as the day he was born. Thereafter he gave himself up to every kind of wickedness you can imagine: fraud, murder, robbery, cards and dice, betrayal, deception… He'd been locked up for four or five years for each, and while doin his time he'd eaten more rope than dinners. And now he was there for spittin in the face of some respected gentleman.

Antonia — What a low-down dirty animal.

Nanna — He was such a scoundrel that sleepin with his mother—which he did—was the least of his sins. And though robbed of all other wealth, he was so rich in the clap he'd enough to share around the whole neighbourhood, and still had a world of it left for himself. There was a doctor hired by the community to treat poor convicts in prison who saw this reprobate, and in the midst of treatin him saw his big auld diddler ripe with sores and cried out: 'I've cured many a man's devilish nature, but I'll be damned if I can put this appendage right!' Well, the blessed nature of this man's organ came to the ear of said woman and its boundless reputation made a home in her bosom, so that she burned for it with more heat than a cow for the bull. Since there was no way or manner she could get rid of her fancy, she came of mind to do somethin to get herself thrown in the same prison. So when Easter came around, she took the communion without confessing, and when the matter was referred to the mayor, he had her seized and bound, upon which she confessed immediately the reason for her transgression. When the wise mayor considered this, he decided that this man, this snake with the eyes of a weasel and a big, scarred and smashed-up nose, ragged, filthy, revolting and infested with nits and lice, and with his big ol' dirty organ all diseased and cankered, the mayor thought this might be the very penance the lady required. He told her: 'This is how you'll pay for your sin *per infinita saeculorum.*' So they threw her in jail, and she was as happy as if she'd just been released. They say that after gettin a taste of that big dirty mickey she said: 'Here we shall build our tabernacles.'

Antonia — So was this burrito as big as a donkey's?

Nanna — Bigger.

Antonia — A mule's?

Nanna — Bigger still.

Antonia — Was he hung like a bull then?

Nanna — More they say.

Antonia — What about a nag?

Nanna — Three times the size, I'm not lyin.

Antonia — Was it as big as one of those walnut bedposts that decorate a four-poster bed?

Nanna — Now you're gettin it.

Antonia — What was your impression of it?

Nanna — While she was gettin stuffed right up to her throat, everyone began to pester the mayor, sayin that, if he really was actin in the interest of justice, he'd send the murderous dog to the gallows. So it was that, ten days hence—but hold on, I just forgot somethin. We'll come back to the rogue. The woman, then... no sooner was she in the jail and her true face was revealed, news of it spread through the town, and gossip was heard from every corner, especially from the women. They talked about nothin else: on the streets, in the windows and on the balconies, they all told their tales, and some of it was met with laughter and some with disgust. And whenever more than a couple of women gathered around the holy water fount, they'd spend hours whisperin about it. One of these little cliques was overheard by a respectable country lady, who said: 'We women are being dishonoured by the shameless conduct of this harlot. We should go the prison and burn her out, then tear her limb from limb. Then we'll stone her, whip her, and hang her upside-down from the cross.' Then she went away, swollen as a wineskin, as if the honour of all the women of the world depended on her.

Antonia — What a muppet.

Nanna — Now when the ten days reprieve was granted to the villain, it came to the ears of this church-goin woman with a stick up her arse, who, as I say, wanted to burn the jail down and drag out the wench. Well, she started to pity the ruffian, and gave mind to all the harm the region would suffer if they lost this man's legendary lumpy cucumber, whose fame drew women like a needle to a magnet. Soon she was taken by the same frenzy for a taste of it the other apostate had, and now she began her own mischievous scheming of which you've never heard the like.

Antonia — I hope to God you never get hot for the mickey like she did, Nanna. What'd she do?

Nanna — This woman had a sick husband, who'd get out of bed for two hours then spend two days sleepin. Sometimes such palpitations came on him he'd choke as if he were about to shuffle off this mortal coil. And since she'd heard that a workin whore might release a man destined for the gallows if she stepped forward and claimed him for her husband—

Antonia — Hold on right there... she what now?

Nanna — You heard right... she resolved to strangle her husband, and with a whore's word take the hanged man as her groom. Just as she was plannin all this, she heard the sick husband cry out: 'Oh Lord God!', and he closed his eyes, clenched his fists, doubled up and fainted. The wife, a big hefty lump of a woman, put a pillow over his mouth and sat on him, and he shat himself and kicked the bucket.

Antonia — Lord save us.

Nanna — Oh, she did make a great racket after that. All the neighbours knew about the man's illness, and when she went to them in distress they'd no doubt he'd taken one of his fits and passed into the hereafter. Since he was rich, he was buried with much honour, and right after this his wife ran off to the whorehouse with a fire between the thighs. No joke. And no one questioned this at all, since they were all convinced she'd been driven crazy by grief. Soon the day of the execution arrived when they were to punish the foul dog. Nearly all the town turned out at the jail to see justice delivered to the man that deserved death a thousand times over. And when he heard the pronouncement, 'It is God's greatest pleasure that you should die', the criminal only laughed. He was taken out between two priests with his feet in the stocks and in handcuffs, and he didn't even glance at the holy image they presented him to kiss. He chatted away and told a hundred stories like he wasn't about to be strung up, and everyone who came to see him he greeted by name. The town bell had been tolling since mornin, proclaiming the coming justice. Then the banners were rolled out and the list of crimes read, which went on almost to evenin. A symbolic rope was slung around his neck and a crown of tinsel paper on his head, which marked him as the king of rascals. And so the trumpets were sounded and he was sent on his way surrounded by policemen, all the townsfolk followin behind. As he passed along, the alleys, roofs and windows were packed with women and children, and all the time he was drawin close to the she-wolf, who was gettin ready to throw herself around the fiend's neck with the same fire as a man with a fever flings himself at a bucket of water. When they came upon the gallows she dashed towards him, parting the crowd with her cries, her hair flyin behind her and arms wavin, and she flung herself at him grippin him tightly and cried, 'I am your wife!' The procession halted and the people trampled each other, and a roar went up. When the news made its way back to the mayor, he was forced to step in and uphold the law, and the man was freed and handed over to the whore, who took him off and wasted no time hangin herself on his gibbet.

Antonia — What has the world come to.

Nanna — Ha ha ha!

Antonia — What are you laughing at?

Nanna — At the woman who turned Lutheran to put herself in the prison, and suffered three times for her pain: once seein him released, once thinkin he was hanged, and once learnin another woman had taken possession of what was hers.

Antonia — God did well when he struck her these three blows.

Nanna — Now, sister, listen to another tale...

Antonia — Gladly.

Nanna — There was this woman who was not uncomely but had no grace about her, not lovely at all but very showy. One of these sorts who pouts her lips and raises an eyebrow at everything. She was a nose-poke, a sniffer out of stenches, the most annoyin creature that ever was born. There wasn't a forehead, an eyelash, a nose or a mouth she didn't have a go at, not a face she didn't find some flaw with. Accordin to her, there wasn't a woman alive knew how to speak or carry herself properly, and every woman she looked at was lumpy and misshapen. If ever she saw a man lookin at one, she'd say, 'Poor girl, she's only the way God made her', and she'd shake her head in pity. She had a poke at the women who hung out their windows as much as those with discretion; everyone ran from this know-it-all as if from bad luck itself. Even in church she'd find complaint: 'Who in the name of God sweeps this place out?' Yes, even the incense stunk in her nostrils. She'd stop at every altar as she was reciting her Our Fathers and say: 'Look at those tablecloths... and the candlesticks!' While the priest was readin the Gospel, she wouldn't stand up like the others but sat with her head turned, as if the priest wasn't even speaking, and when he raised the host she'd say: 'It isn't even made with good flour', and dippin a finger in the holy water she'd proclaim, 'You think they'd change it once in a while'. And no matter how many men she met, she'd say to a one: 'Look at those skinny legs, he's like a chicken.' 'What fat feet!' 'What a ghoul.' 'He has the face of a dog.' But this witch, who wanted people to praise her for havin what others lacked, one day laid eyes on a monk who came to knock on her door for bread. Since he was a well-cut young man with a strong back and without a care, she fell head over heels for him. Sayin that charity should come from the hand of the mistress and not the servants, she ran straight to the larder to ply the monk with scran. When her husband said, 'Let the maid bring it to him,' she argued with him for an hour about what real charity was, and the difference between giving of her own hand and from that of others. She soon became intimate with this eater of gruel who'd bring her the *Agnus Dei,* and it wasn't long before they reached an agreement.

Antonia — What was the bargain?

Nanna — That she'd run away to the monastery.

Antonia — How exactly?

Nanna — Dressed as a little brother. And to put the blame on her husband so she'd have an excuse to flee, one day she tried to convince him the feast of Our Lady fell on August sixteenth. She made him so mad he took her by the neck and twisted it, and would've pulled it off like a chicken's if her mother hadn't dragged her from his hand.

Antonia — What a pig-headed jezebel.

Nanna — She got to her feet and began to shout: 'So that's the way it is, eh? Wait til my brothers hear about this. You'd slap around a woman, eh? Try it with a man and see how it goes. I'm not takin it anymore, I'm off to the convent—I'd rather eat grass than suffer you a moment longer. Maybe I'll even throw myself in the shithouse, cause if I don't see your face again I'll die contented!' Sobbin and sighin, she sat down with her head between her knees, and would've stayed that way til

70

mornin had her mother not taken her away, pullin her twice from the clutches of her husband, who wanted to wring her neck. Now, about that monk—he was about thirty, sinewy, full of life, big and brawny, cheerful, and a friend to everyone. The next day he came for his alms, knockin on the door when the husband was gone, shoutin: 'Bread for the monks?' The grateful woman ran to him and they agreed to flee the followin day at dawn. Then Fra Fazio—that was his name—went off. He showed up an hour before dawn the next day, gettin there even before the baker. The dainty madam got up quickly, sayin to herself: *You can't dirty your hands with your own shit.* Then she kicked the maid's door. 'Get up and get to it,' she said, and went down the stairs and let the brother in. Then, takin off the dress she'd flung on her and hangin it over the well, she took a robe the monk had brought and put it on, and pullin the door closed behind her she fled, and not a soul saw her go. And once at the monastery the monk led her to his cell and enjoyed his oats. First he laid her out on the pallet slung with an old pilgrim's robe, a rotten old thing that stank of shit. Then, puffin and blowin, he lifted up his habit and went at her with the fury of the August storm that shakes the olive tree, and the big monk shook it so hard the cell around them almost came down. A cheap Madonna on the wall trembled and fell, and all the while our little lady friar was howlin and scratchin like an alley cat. In good time, her companion spilled his holy wine into her chalice.

Antonia — You mean his 'seed'. Speak straight, for the other day when I was speakin to the mother of that whore, Mamma-Don't-Wan'-It, I was told off for sayin 'moan', 'gushing', and 'startled'.

Nanna — Why's that?

Antonia — Because she says she's been taught to speak properly, and her daughter is the finest at it.

Nanna — What the hell does she mean, 'speak properly'?

Antonia —You have to say 'opening' and not 'window', 'portal' and not 'door', 'visage' and not 'face', 'heart organ' and not 'ticker', 'harvest' and not 'crops', 'knock' and not 'bang'… As you've told me, I dunno how many times, she misses nothin. The way I see it, the students of this school want to rewrite the book.

Nanna — Screw these gobshites. I'll say what I want, and I learned everything I know from the cunt that shit me out. And if I want to say 'gab' and not 'talk', I'll say it. 'Bullshit' and not 'inanity'—at least I'll be talkin like they do where I grew up. Ach, what a load of old twat. Back to the monk. He dipped his beak twice into Miss Nose-In-The-Air without takin his eel from her slippery clam.

Antonia — Ah. We're back to normal.

Nanna — Havin emptied his bag, he locked her in the cell, stuffin her under his bed. He had to go out beggin bread, since now he had two mouths to feed, and it wasn't long before he wandered back to her house to see what had happened since she'd left. No sooner did he appear than a stink was kicked up in the house, and the mother and the maidservants appeared in the window shoutin: 'Bring the grapple!' 'Bring the rope!'

Antonia — Why grapple? Why rope?

Nanna — Because after noticing the ditso wasn't there, the mother called and shouted for her, and looked for her here, there, everywhere and all over, then they saw the slippers and the robe on the wall of the well and became convinced she'd thrown herself in. The mother shouted 'Help!' and the whole neighbourhood showed up to fish her out. It was a shame to see the poor old woman throw the grapple, sayin, 'Pull yourself up, child, sweet child, your good mother's here!' And after: 'Oh the thief, the traitor, the Judas Iscariot!' But not a bloody thing did she fish out of the well.

Antonia — Say 'nothing', if you want to speak in the correct way.

Nanna — She fished out nothin and flung away the grapple in desperation. Then she crossed her hands and raised her face to the sky, and said, 'Is it fair, Dear God, that a daughter so wise, so adventurous, and so without sin, should come to such an end? My prayers and implications have turned against me! Strike me dead if I ever light another candle again.' Then she caught sight of the friar, who was mingling among the crowd, smirking at the old woman's laments, and thinkin he'd come for flour and suspecting no involvement with her daughter, she grabbed him by the scapular and dragged him into the open, and sent forth a tirade against him and against God who'd failed her daughter. 'You filthy plate-licker! Soup-for-brains, Pappa lasagna, wine-swiller, fart-puller, pig-scratcher, Lent-breaker!' and many other curses did she hurl and which made everyone gasp. Some old witches in the crowd said they remembered when the well was dug and that it had so many tunnels goin this way and that, that certainly she was stuck in one of em. On hearing this, the mother cried: 'O my daughter, you'll starve down there and I'll never see your beauty, grace and virtue again!' She offered the world to any who'd dive the well for her, but to a one they were terrified of the tunnels the old women had told of. So they turned their backs on her and went with God.

Antonia — What happened to the husband?

Nanna — He got on like a cat with a roasted tail. He didn't even have the gall to show his face, because it was bandied about everywhere it was his evil ways had caused her to fling herself down the hole. He was also afraid of the mother-in-law, that she'd put his eyes out. But he couldn't avoid her totally, and when she came upon him she'd scream, 'Traitor, are you happy now? Your drinking and whoring have drowned my daughter, my only consolation in this world. Wear a crucifix around your neck, if you know what's good for you, because I'm going to have you cut into little pieces! Doesn't matter where you hide, you'll get what's coming to you, you degenerate, you murderer!' The poor man, he looked like one of those terrified women who stick their fingers in their ears when they hear a musket blast. Leavin the old woman to drown in her poison, he locked himself in his bedroom, pondering what had happened to his wife, for there was somethin strange to him about the whole affair. The mother was crazed and continued to hover around the well like an altar, and all the icons she had in the house were hung around it, and she burned ten years' worth of holy candles in supplication, and every mornin stood next to it and said a rosary for the soul of her daughter.

Antonia — What'd the friar do after being dragged by the scapular?

Nanna — He returned to his cell where his little fox was still hidin under the bed, and he told her the whole sordid tale and they howled at the affair, like those who howled at the antics of our good Master Andrea of Strascino, God give him peace.

Antonia — For sure, his death was a great loss to Rome. We've been widowed; no longer do we know carnivals or good entertainment.

Nanna — And just imagine if we lost Rosso. His jests are miraculous. But back to the friar. He was a full month goin walkin day and night for seven, eight, nine miles in search of food. Still, he never failed to manage to slip into his lady's foxhole at night, erect and full of vigour.

Antonia — How'd he feed her?

Nanna — With whatever he could get his hands on. Because he was keepin the monastery in provisions, he'd go to the farmyards and kitchens of the peasants and come back with a loaded donkey three times a week, wood too, and bread for the friars and oil for the lamps, and since he procured everything himself he was master of it all. He also liked to work the lathe, and made decent money churnin out spinning tops for children and pestles and spindles, and got a tiny percentage of every candle burned in the cemetery on All Soul's Day. The cooks gave him first refusal of the head, feet and the innards of the chickens. Now this friar the woman idolised—placing her body in heaven by turning over care of her soul—he awakened the gardener's suspicions by pickin certain salad greens that normally he never touched; so the gardener kept a keen eye on him and noticed the weight was fallin off him, with the eyes sunken and a haggard look about his jowl, staggerin when he walked, always with fresh eggs in his hand, so the gardener says to himself: 'Somethin's up...' He mentioned this to the bell-ringer, and the bell-ringer mentioned it to the cook, the cook to the Sacristan and the Sacristan to the Prior, and the Prior to the Provincial and the Provincial to the General. A spy was set watch on his cell, and when he went out on his perambulations they unlocked his room and found the woman. 'Come out of there!' they called, and she came out with a face on her like a witch to the pyre. And when the brother returned they summoned him, tied him up, and marked him out for some dastardly punishment. They threw him into a dark dungeon which was flooded a foot deep with water, givin him a slice of semolina bread in the mornin and one in the evenin, with a glass of watered-down vinegar and half a head of garlic. Disputing what was to be done about the woman, some said, 'Let's bury her alive', and others, 'Let them die in the dungeon together'. Others were more pitiful. 'Let us return her to her own', one said, and another wise man: 'Let's enjoy her a few days, then God will inspire us'. At this proposal all the young'uns laughed, and even a few older ones. Some of the old men sneered. In the end they decided to see how many men it would take to till this particular field, and once the ruling was made, the strumpet even grinned to find out she was to be the hen at the rooster party. When the time came, the General dutifully took her in hand, and after him the Provincial, then the Prior, and all the way down to the bell-ringer and the gardener she was passed hand to hand, each of them havin a shake at the walnut tree, shakin it so eagerly the woman shone like a cherry, and for a whole two days these sparrows did nothin but flutter in and out of the hayloft. After a few days the dungeon was opened and the prisoner came out, and he forgave them all and agreed to have his property consigned to the common pot, and enjoy it together with his fathers and brothers. Would you believe it, she took that grinding for a whole year.

Antonia — Why wouldn't I believe it?

Nanna — She would've stayed there forever if she hadnt've gotten knocked up and gave birth to this dog-like monster, which quite pissed off the monks.

Antonia — Why?

Nanna — Cause her gash gaped so wide after shittin out the beastly abomination. Awful thing. The monks made some necromantic computations, and decided the watchdog that guarded the vegetable garden had mounted her.

Antonia — Is that even possible?

Nanna — I'm only tellin it to you as I heard it from everyone else, who saw it dead after the monks had murdered it.

Antonia — And what was done to the dirty slut after she'd given birth?

Nanna — She gave herself up to the husband, or rather her mother, with the most beautiful cunning in the world.

Antonia — Tell me.

Nanna — Among those monks was one who exorcised evil spirits, and one night he climbed the wall of this woman's house onto the roof, and by the Devil, slipped inside. He went to the room of the mother who was awake and wailin in the dark for her daughter, and hearin her cry out, 'My girl, where are you?', he replied, putting on her voice: 'In a safe place. And alive, thanks to your rosaries, Mama. Ten days from now you'll see me fatter and healthier than ever'. Leavin her stricken, he left. He went back to the monastery and told the monks of his cunning, then they called for the woman. On behalf of all there the Prior thanked the woman for her generosity and begged her forgiveness for not havin done everything in their power to restore her good spirits. Then he dressed her in a white gown and put a crown of olives on her head, and two hours before daybreak sent her home with the friar who'd whispered of her return to the old mother, who'd been resurrected by her 'vision' and was waitin expectantly for the return. Once there, she took leave of the friar and sat down by the well. Next thing, day broke. The maid, gettin up from the bed, went out to fetch the water, and seein her mistress there dressed like Holy Ursula, cried out: 'Miracle! It's a miracle!' The mother flew down the stairs and outside, and hurled herself at her daughter in such joy that she almost sent the poor girl down the well for real. The word spread and mayhem ensued, and hordes rushed to the site of the miracle the way they do when they find a weeping Madonna. The husband was one of em too. He threw himself at her feet, and not being able to say the *miserere* for the weepin, threw out his arms in supplication as if he'd just received the stigmata. The woman raised him up and kissed him, and she told them all the story of how she'd survived in the well, goin so far as to recount how the Sibyl of Norcia and the Fata Morgana lived down there too. This caused a commotion, and many of the old women were ready to throw themselves in. But what more can I say? The well made such a name for itself that a gridiron was put over it, and any woman who had an angry husband flocked there to drink its waters, and it seemed to help too. Any woman who was gettin married began to pray to it also, and begged the faeries of the well to bring them good fortune. In one year there were more candles, more robes and more camisoles, and more holy icons around this well than there are around the burial of blessed saint Lena dal Olio in Bologna.

Antonia — She was another lunatic.

Nanna — Don't take her name in vain, or you'll be excommunicated. I dunno which Cardinal raked in the money by canonising her, but I know she was consort of the friar who purified the devotees of the Blessed Vastalla.

Antonia — May he live for a hundred years.

Nanna — I could go on forever about married women, so I'll wrap up by tellin ya the one about the woman with the most handsome husband in the world, who fell in love with one of these wandering merchants who go about with a haberdashery board about their neck, shoutin: 'Beautiful ribbons, needles, pins and thimbles! Mirrors, combs and scissors!' Always bartering with this or that housewife over oils and soaps for bread, rags and old shoes, and always wheedlin a couple of coins to boot. The woman became so smitten with him that she shat on her honour and even gave her worldly belongings to him, and this rag-

and-bone man got a bit up himself, dressed himself up like a knight
and began to weasel in with the nobility. Soon people were doffing
their caps to him. He really deserved a crown.

Antonia — Why?

Nanna — Because he treated the source of his wealth the way one
treats a common tart. Not only did he take a club to her, but he
bragged in public about what he did.

Antonia — Oh aye...

Nanna — But these are merely tidbits, these stories I've told you. The
really incredible things happen among the ladies and the gentlemen.
If they wouldn't brand me an evil gossip, I could tell you about those
who give themselves to the footman, the steward, the stable boy and
the cook. Even the scullion.

Antonia — Stay in the saddle, girl. Tell me all.

Nanna — So long as you believe me.

Antonia — Come on now. Spill it.

Nanna — Ach, Antonia...

Antonia — I'm takin it all in, Nanna.

Nanna — Remember, the stories I told you about the nuns were only
what I saw in a few days, and in one convent, and as regards the wives,
only a fraction of what I saw in a single town. Imagine what goes on
among all the nuns in Christendom, or all the wives in all the cities of
the world.

Antonia — Is it possible the good ones are, like you say, like coins: Be
wise and take them on faith?

Nanna — Maybe.

Antonia — Even Franciscans?

Nanna — I'm not talkin about them. I'm tellin ya, the prayers they
send up for the depraved nuns are the reason the Devil doesn't swallow
em whole, shoes and all; their virginity is as sweet-smellin as the
whoredom of the others stinks, and God Almighty is beside them day
and night, even as the Devil is beside the others in their wakin and

sleepin. It would bode ill for us if we didn't have the prayers of the saints. Ill for us, I tell you. And it's true that those few good nuns there are among the cloistered are so good, so perfect, that we should burn candles at their feet like we do the Blessed Madonna.

Antonia — You're fair. You don't speak flippantly.

Nanna — There are also some very good wives who'd sooner let themselves be flayed like St. Bartholomew than let anyone touch their little finger.

Antonia — This makes me happy. If you consider the poverty into which we women are born, this is reason enough to do what men tell us to do. Not because we're bad like people say.

Nanna — You're not hearin me—I'm tellin you, we're born flesh and we die flesh; the prick makes us, and the prick is our undoing. And to show you you're wrong, think of the ladies with pearls and golden necklaces and glittering rings to throw away, who behave like beggar women in the face of a stud. For each woman that likes her husband there's a thousand that are disgusted with theirs. For every two people who make bread under their own roof, there are hundreds who want the baker's because it's whiter.

Antonia — Aye, I hand it to you.

Nanna — And I accept. Now let's finish it. Female chastity is like a crystal decanter... no matter the care with which you handle it, in the end it slips from your hand and smashes, right when you least expect it. It's impossible to keep it intact, unless you're lockin it up in a chest. The woman who does so is kind of miraculous, like glass that falls and doesn't shatter.

Antonia — I see your logic.

Nanna — To conclude, once I'd seen what the life of a wife was really about, I had to have some for myself, so I went about cavorting and satisfying my every whim; I wanted to have a go at the porters, I wanted to try the lords, and above all, the friars, the monks and the priests. And it thrilled me greatly that my husband not only knew about it, but saw it too. I heard some about me whisper: 'He's getting his just desserts. Good for her'. Once when he tried to have a go at me for it, with total cruelty I dug my nails into his head and ripped out his hair. I said: 'Who do you think you're talkin to, you dirty old wretch!' And I never let up on him. Soon I shook him out of his usual stupor and brought the rage out in him.

Antonia — Nanna, don't you know what they say? If you want to make a man valiant, you must first make a villain of him.

Nanna — Well, that's how he became valiant, because I did just as you say. He swallowed betrayal after betrayal like burning coals, watchin every one with his own eyes, until one day he came home and found a beggar ridin on me. Well, he couldn't swallow that, and he tried to smash up my face. I twisted from his grip and pulled out a small knife which I carried, angry he'd interrupted me. I stuck it in him and his heart stopped.

Antonia — May God forgive him.

Nanna — When my mother found out about it, she sold everything we had and we fled here to Rome. What came after, I'll tell you all about it tomorrow. I'm done for today. Let's get up and go get dinner. I'm thirsty from so much chattering, and I'm so hungry I can barely stand.

Antonia — Oh Jaysus, the cramp in my foot!

Nanna — Make the sign of the cross on it with spit and it'll go away.

Antonia — Done.

Nanna — Did it help?

Antonia — My God, it's gone away.

Nanna — Let's go home then. You'll stay with me tonight.

Antonia — We'll put it on the tab.

Nanna locked the gate of the vineyard and they went all the way home without another word. They reached there at dusk with the sun disappearing, and the cicadas giving way to the crickets. Already the owls and the bats were revealing themselves to the grave and melancholy night, and the masked moon sidled out onstage. The stars, gilded with fire by Master Apollo, appeared at the window: one, two, four and fifty, a hundred and a thousand... They resembled roses, that upon daybreak open one by one, lighted by the rays of the Master Poet. Or perhaps like an army coming into an open field, first ten, then twenty, then behold the multitude, scattered across the land. But maybe the reader will not like this comparison; today soup cannot be stomached without first being sweetened by herbs. Nevertheless, Nanna and Antonia, having arrived and done what needed to be done, bedded down to rest until the next day.

*Here ends the second day
of the whimsical Dialogues of Aretino.*

HERE BEGINS

the third day of the whimsical Dialogues
of Pietro Aretino, in which Nanna tells Antonia
of the life of Whores.

Day was upon them when the two women were getting out of bed. Taking a large basket they filled it with food they'd prepared the day before, gave it to the maid, and sent her ahead with a flagon of wine. Antonia carried a tablecloth and napkins under her arm so they could eat like civilised women. When they got to the vineyard, Antonia put the cloth on a large flat stone that lay beneath a shelter next to a well, and the maid opened the basket, laying out the salt and the napkins and the knives. Since the sun was coming up they hurried to finish so they wouldn't have to share breakfast with him, finishing up with a ball of mozzarella. They left the maid to wolf the leftovers, and Nanna told her: 'Be sure and take everything back.' Then the two women took a stroll around the vineyard, before returning and sitting down under the fig tree. After resting a little while, Antonia said:

I thought as I was gettin dressed it'd be a fine thing if someone wrote down all your stories about the life of the priests and monks and the friars, so the women who read about it could have a good auld giggle like we have these past two days. Just like these men like to have a laugh at us to make themselves seem wise. I swear, it's like I can hear the stories bein read already. I dunno who's writin them down, but my ears are burnin, so it must be true.

Nanna — Maybe you're right. But let's get to how my mother brought me to Rome.

Antonia — Go on then.

Nanna — I remember it well. We arrived on the eve of St. Peter's Day. God knows I took pleasure in the fireworks and the fires which burned furiously around the castle, and the sound of the bagpipes and the crowds in the Ponte and Borgo districts.

Antonia — Where did you stay when you first got there?

Nanna — In Torre di Nona, in a dark room above an inn. We were there about eight days. Then the landlady of the house, who was mad about me cause I looked so pretty, let slip about me to some gigolo. The next day, you should've seen the men who came by to ogle and rubberneck, and they cursed my mother for not lettin them see me. I watched from behind the shutter, peekin out now and again and bangin it shut when their eyes turned on me. Yes, I was beautiful, and givin em a tiny flash of my charms made me even more alluring. Of course, this made them want to see me even more; soon the chat was all over Rome about this comely young stranger who'd appeared among them. People always like somethin different and new, as you know, so they queued up to get a squint at me, and the landlady wasn't left alone for a minute. I'm sure they promised her everything if she'd only hand me over. My wise old mother—who taught me everything I know and ever will—wouldn't hear a word of it. 'Think I'm gonna marry her off to one of those degenerates? God forbid my daughter should suffer such a misfortune—I'm a good woman, and even if we've suffered, we've enough left, by God, to get by.' Of course, this only served to increase my worth even more. Ever seen a sparrow in the window of a barn? He pecks a couple of grains of wheat then flies away. Next time, he comes back with two others, then four, then ten. Soon there's thirty of em, then a whole cloud. That's what it was like with these libertines swarmin the house, tryin to dip their beaks in my font; but I couldn't stop lookin. I almost went dizzy peerin through the blinds, watchin them in their velvet and satin and with medals in their caps and chains around their necks, some on their steeds holdin Petrarch in their hands and singin out the verses.

Antonia — Oh, swoon. If that's not love, then I don't know what is...

Nanna — Now and again they'd halt in front of the window where I was peekin and say, 'Madam, are you so cruel as to let your admirers die of love?' At this I'd slam the shutter and run back inside, chuckling. Then they'd shout: 'Your lordship places a thousand kisses on your hand!' or, 'By God, you are so cruel!'

Antonia — Such beautiful things they say.

Nanna — Things being so, one day my mother decided to make a little show of me, letting on it was entirely capricious. She dressed me in a sleeveless robe of peacock satin and tied up my hair just so; you'd have sworn it wasn't hair but a skein of spun gold.

Antonia — Why did she put you in a sleeveless dress?

Nanna — Because my arms were white as snowflakes. And she made me wash my face with a certain eau de toilette of hers but without any shameful make-up, and put me in the window when outside was swarmin with gigolos. And thus I appeared to them like a star to the Magi; they abandoned their horses and rejoiced. They gazed at me, staring enraptured like prisoners at the sunlight. Like those little foreign animals that live on nothing but air.

Antonia — You mean chameleons.

Nanna — That's the one. Those googly-eyed things. They impregnated me with their stares, like those birds that look like sparrow hawks, the ones that seem to impregnate the clouds with their feathers.

Antonia — Nighthawks?

Nanna — By God, you're right again.

Antonia — What were you doin while they were all googling at you?

Nanna — I put on the airs of a nun, stared with the assurance of a wife, and had the thoughts of a whore.

Antonia — You cheeky little thing…

Nanna — After standin there for almost an hour my mother appeared at the window and made me leave. They were left gasping and gaping like fish pulled from the water, leapin about like barbels hoisted out by the net. That night, we heard a gentle rapping on the door. Comes down the mistress to the fellow wrapped in his hood while my mother stood listenin, and the fellow said: 'Who was she in front of the window earlier?' The landlady answered: 'The daughter of a good woman from the country. Her father was murdered and the poor woman fled here with her only possessions.' All these little fibs my mother had told her.

Antonia — Smart.

Nanna — Hearin this, the disguised man says to her: 'Can I have a word with the good woman?' 'Out of the question,' she replies. 'She wants nothing to do with you.' And bein asked in a whisper if I was a virgin, she replies to him, 'Pure as the driven snow. The girl lives on Hail Marys.' 'He who munches on Hail Marys will spit out Our Fathers,' the man said and sneered, and tried to push his way inside. The landlady blocked his way. Then the rake says, 'Do me a favour, then—tell her when she's ready to give a man a chance, I'll give her something she'll be thanking me for forever more.' Swearin she would, she chased him off and came back up the stairs to us. 'One thing you can count on,' she says, 'no one but a drunk knows where to find the best wine. These foxes have sniffed out your daughter like a quail… one of them was here just now. He asks for an audience with her.' 'Not on your life,' my mother replies. 'No, no, no.' And the landlady who had a serpentine tongue, says to her: 'A smart woman knows when to grab fortune when God sends it her way. That there's a man can shower you with gold!' Tellin the landlady she'd think about it, my mother sent her on. The woman laid it on thick the next day by puttin out a full table for us, and my mother, too shrewd a householder, soon came around to her way of thinkin. So she promised to let this man, who thought he was a cut above the rest, say his piece. When he was summoned and arrived at the house, after offerin a thousand assurances he put down a security on my virginity, promising me the world from Rome to Rio.

Antonia — Score.

Nanna — To get to the point, the day came, and after a banquet in which I got to enjoy about eight bites of food and a mouthful of wine, without a word I was led to the landlady's bedroom, who'd let us have it for a night in exchange for a ducat. I was barely through the door when he locked it shut, and he'd the clothes aff him in the blink of an eye. He leapt in the sack and let forth a sickly-sweet tirade: 'I'll make a woman of you, and I'll give you so much you'll be the envy of the finest whore in Rome.' Still, I refused to be buttered up. I put up such a fight he jumped from the bed, ripped off my stockings, and still I put up stiff resistance. Gettin into bed eventually, he turned to face the wall so I wouldn't be ashamed to be seen in my camisole. As I reached for the lamp he said: 'Don't do it!', but I put it out all the same. He was on me with more desperation than a mother throws herself on the body of her dead son. He clasped me tight and kissed me. I wriggled and squirmed to show that I was submitting unwillingly, then he took my hand and put it on his harp—which was well-tuned and already taut—as he groped my peach. But when he tried to stick the starfruit in the snatch, I tightened up like a clam. Then he says: 'My soul, my sweetheart, lie still—if I hurt you, you can kill me.' So I stood firm as he pleaded and swore, all the while givin me sly pokes of the langer, testin the walls until he was knackered. Then he took it and put it in my hand: 'Right then, you take it and put it in yourself. I won't move a muscle.' I was almost weepin. 'What is this big nasty thing?' I said. 'Do other men have big ugly things like this? You want to split me in two, do you?' And I lay there like wood and let him poke about, and just when he was about to jam it in I'd pull away and leave him drippin with passion. Then he got desperate and began to pray. And got nasty too: 'Good God, I'll strangle you and drown you.' He grabbed me by the throat and squeezed, then he came at me from another angle and told me to lie so, still tryin to cut the muffin with the knife and still not gettin it in. Then he got up and put on his nightshirt, and as he was goin I grabbed him by the arm. 'Wait, wait... come back. I'll do exactly as you wish.' He cooled off then. Then he gave me a kiss and said: 'You won't feel any more than a fly's nibble. Wait and see—I'll be nice and gentle.' So at last I let him put in about a third of his tadge and not a millimetre more. He lost it and crumpled down by the side of the bed, ass in the air and with his head between his knees, and with the urgency he wanted to unleash upon me he relieved himself with the hand. Then he got up, got dressed, and paced the room the night long. And in the mornin, with a face on him like a long drink, lookin like a gambler who'd lost everything and his sleep besides, he cursed and went to the window and, with his head in his hands, just stared out at the Tiber, which seemed to be laughin at him for the fury with which he'd slapped the salami. I slept like a baby. When I opened my eyes and went to get up, he leapt on me like a thief, and I don't know if any sorcerer ever summoned so many devils and demons as he called down upon my head, but it was all in vain. In the end he begged for a single kiss, and I even denied him that. Hearin my mother chat downstairs with the landlady, I called her up. He opened the bedroom door to her and said: 'What kind of skullduggery is this? I'd be treated better in a den of thieves.' The landlady tried to comfort him, sayin: 'Don't you know it's murder trying to do it with a virgin?' I got dressed and went to my room, and left him crabbing on at the lady. The poor fellow... he was tryin to win back his losses. So he went out, and about an hour later a tailor arrived with a length of green silk and took my measurements to cut me a dress, the fellow believin that, if I accepted his gift, the next night everything would go his way. On seein the present, my mother said: 'His piston's a-pumpin... be strong and he'll give you everything

you want—a house, furniture, yes, by God he will, or he'll die tryin.'
But even without her words I would've known what to do. I looked
out the window into the street. Seein him there, I ran down the stairs
to meet him. 'God knows how much I suffered when you left without
saying goodbye,' I cried, 'but now that you're back, my heart rejoices.
Tonight, I'll do whatever you want, even if it kills me.' His mouth fell
open and he kissed me wildly. And over dinner that night, he was very
peaceful and jolly. When night came—and for him the wait must have
been pure torture—we returned to bed, and findin me as compliant as
a Jewish moneylender without collateral for a loan, he got so angry he
smacked me about. I put up with it, sayin to myself: 'You'll get what's
comin to you.' I kept him at it for hours, until he gave up and squeezed
the spitstick, spillin his seed, after which he got up and flew to where
my mother was sleepin with the landlady to shout and squabble. 'Sir,
be patient,' my mother said, 'tomorrow you'll get what you want,
even if it kills her.' Then she got up and give him a length of taffeta.
'Tomorrow night, tie her hands with this.' The oaf took it, and after
buyin dinner again took me to bed the next night. This time, when
I wouldn't let him even touch me, he got so angry he pulled out his
dagger. Honest to God, by now I was scared, but I turned my back to
him and pressed against him, locking his wallopstick against his belly.
This got him mad horny again, so he began pokin about, lookin for an
entry point, but I lay there stiff and unmoving until he fell away. And
when he tried to force it in, I cried out: 'It's time to get up!' and slid
away. He pinned me on my back again, climbed on me and managed
to get it in about halfway, and I shouted, 'It hurts, it hurts!' As he was
holdin the position like a soldier, he slipped his hand under the pillow,'
took out his purse and pulled out ten ducats and I don't know how
many julios, and pressed them into my hand. 'Take it,' he said. 'No!' I
cried. 'I don't want them!' At the same time I grabbed his chub in my
fist and wouldn't let it in more than half in. Not being able to ram it in
further, he spat out his soul.

Antonia — Why didn't he tie you up with the belt?

Nanna — Because he was all tied up by me.

Antonia — You speak the Gospel truth.

Nanna — His horse went four more times to the half-halt before mornin.

Antonia — Just like Petrarch said.

Nanna — Dante it was.

Antonia — Not Petrarch?

Nanna — Dante, my dear. Anyway, he was content with what he'd managed. He got up and I lay on. Since he couldn't stay to eat with us, he sent out for food and returned again that evenin with supper.

Antonia — Hold on just a minute—didn't he notice you didn't bleed?

Nanna — Ah, you're on the ball. These playboys know all about virgins! In the dark, I convinced him my piss was blood, and anyway, so long as they can jam it in there, they're happy. Now on the fourth night I let him put the whole thing in, and when he felt it go in, he almost passed out. In the mornin my mother came in, laughin to see us in bed together, and she gave me her blessing, greeting his lordship. And as I was coverin him with sweet kisses, she said: 'Tomorrow I'm leavin Rome. I've received a letter from the village and I want to return to die among my own. Rome is not for the adventurous, and not for those without the blessing of an income; certainly I would never leave if I could sell our possessions and buy a little house here. I thought I could rent one, but we simply don't have the money, and I'm not the kind of woman to sleep in other people's rooms.' At which I cried out: 'Mama, but I'll die if I am separated from my beloved!' And I gave him a kiss and let the tears fall. At this point he sat up in bed and said: 'I'll rent a house for you with everything you need. I swear it, by our little whore here.' Gettin dressed in a shot, he dashed from the house and came home in the evenin with a key in his hand and with two porters laden with mattresses and blankets, two others with beds and tables, and I dunno how many Jews behind with upholstery, sheets, buckets, pots, and a whole lot else besides. Then he took my mother away to the sweet little house right by the river, and came back to me, paid the landlady of the house, put all our possessions on a cart, and as dusk fell he drove me there. As long as we were together, he spent a good deal of what he had on me, I mean it. Now that I no longer appeared at the window like before, it soon became known where I'd gone, and they began reappearing about me, like bees to the flower. I took one as a lover on sight, who said he was dyin on my account. I strung him along through a ruffian friend of his, and once he began to shower me with possessions, I turned my back on my first lover, who'd borrowed all around him and bought everything he'd given to me on credit, and when he failed to pay up his debts he was excommunicated with the devils and his name made public for all to see, as per the custom in Rome. And as for this new one, since I was now a whore proper, I began to ration out my lovemaking as his gifts slowed. Soon after he began to find my door locked, and would bawl through it about all the good he'd done me, until eventually he departed like a ghost, his tail between his legs. Then I found a third. In short, I gave myself to those who showed up at my door with the silver, as Gonnella said, took two maids and lived in a big house like a proper lady. And don't think that in refining my whoredom I was like one of these scholars who turns up at the university to study, and after seven years returns home broke. In three months—less, actually... two, or even one—I learned everything one can about torturing a man then makin it up to him, then gettin him to open his purse, and as suddenly leavin him, and about cryin with laughter and in laughter, cryin... I sold my cherry more times than one of those priests who announces his first mass, putting up posters everywhere indicatin he's going to deliver it. I'll tell you only a fraction of the swindles—which in truth is what they are—that I've done to men; and those I'll tell you about are my own and no one else's. So get ready, and I'll fill you up like a wine flask.

Antonia — I'm certainly no wine flask, but feel free to dispense.

Nanna — There was one man among all my lovers who had a hold on me, but to be honest, a whore knows no obligation, only coin. A whore's love is like a termite: the more it eats, the more determined it becomes. But when the man goes out the door, the Devil take him. Now this lover of mine, I did play some weird games with, and did it more so even as he began to tighten the purse strings, yet I wangled it from him all the same. He was my Friday fella. As soon as he arrived at mine for dinner, I would ball him out.

Antonia — Why?

Nanna — To give him a gippy belly.

Antonia — Aw, now that's cruel.

Nanna — He had it comin. So, after demolishing dinner, I'd drag my feet for an hour or two before goin to bed. Then, when I eventually got in, I tore into him so savagely he'd roll off me, curse the day he was baptised, and refuse to ride me. Then, in the end, burstin with the horn, he'd relent, but I'd refuse to touch him. Then he'd shake me like a ragdoll with tears in his eyes and curse me and call me the filthiest names, and after that when he wanted to throw the leg over I demanded he hand over every coin in his purse before I opened my legs.

Antonia — What a monster. Like Nero, but a woman.

Nanna — As for the merchants from out of town who came to stay a week or ten days in Rome before leavin, I used to fleece em clean. I had a couple of bad boys workin tricks for me, and in return I gave em a free ride once in a blue moon. So these merchants who came to Rome usually wanted to see the sights, and that included the ladies. They wanted to play 'lord of the manor' if you get what I mean. I was always the first to receive a visit from these fellas, and the man that spent the night with me usually left without his clothes.

Antonia — How the hell did he go without the clothes?

Nanna — I'll tell ya. So in the mornin the maid comes into my room and takes the man's clothes, sayin she's gonna clean em. Then she'd hide em and begin shoutin that they'd been stolen. The good fellow, pullin himself out of bed in his undershirt, would then demand his things, threatening to smash up the house. Then I would shout loudly and say, 'You'll smash up my house, will you, beat me around in my own house? Are you callin me a thief?' Hearin this, my ruffians, who were hidin downstairs, ran up with their swords drawn. 'What's goin on, ma'am?' they'd shout. Then they grab him by the scruff, him standin there in the nightshirt lookin like a penitent, and he'd beg my forgiveness and ask for a friend who might lend him pants and a shirt. Then he'd go on his way, feelin lucky he hadn't tasted the point of a sword.

Antonia — Ah, but how did your heart take it. I couldn't.

Nanna — Easily. Because there's no cruelty, treachery or thievery that's too much for a whore. Anyway, when word got about, those men stopped visitin my house, or if they came, first gave their best clothes to a servant who took them to their lodgings and came back in the mornin to dress them. Despite this, there was always one who left his gloves, or belt, or cap... because a whore knows how to make a turn of everything: a ribbon, a needle, a cherry, a head of fennel, right down to the peel of a pear!

Antonia — Even so, I bet for all their cunning, some of them whores are reduced to sellin candles. I'm sure the clap gets them in the end too. It's really somethin to see one of those old pros past her prime, no longer able to hide her age behind strong colognes and fine dresses and fans, and has to pawn off her necklaces, rings and good silks. Then she's forced to go nun, just like a young boy who wants to become a priest.

Nanna — What do you mean?

Antonia — I mean first she offers sanctuary to all comers by turnin her fleshy delights into a bed, then when she's run her course she becomes a tavernkeeper, and from that, a brothel madam, and when she's burnt out at that game she's reduced to washin linen. In the end, she's beggin on the steps of St. Peter's and St. John's... by then she's been stigmatised and maybe had a few cuts across the nose with a wayward blade from customers who got tired of her swindles.

Nanna — I have never been one of those. A whore without brains is her own undoing. You've gotta know how to hold yourself up in this world but not try to make a queen of yourself, openin your door only to lords and gentlemen. The greatest mountain is that which is built little by little, and often; a thousand flies shit as much as an ox, and there are more flies than oxen. For every lord who enters your house with a little gift there are twenty loaded with promises, and yet a thousand men who are no lords will fill your hands to overflowing. She's mad, the woman who only takes in those dressed in velvet. And I know well, the best tippers are the innkeepers, the chicken-pickers, the water-carriers, the stall-keepers and the Jews. These men go to the front of the queue, because they spend more than they steal. Fancy clothes are often nothin but deception.

Antonia — Why's that then?

Nanna — Why? Because those fancy silken pants hide nasty debts, and most playboys are like snails who wear their worldly belongings on their backs. Everything else is smoke and air. What little coin they have goes to oil for greasin their beards, and for the one pair of fine shoes they flaunt they've a hundred that are stripped to the sole. Aye, they can turn miracles with a good shirt, but it isn't long before they're threadbare.

Antonia — You're used to these misers of today. In my time they were different, for the stinginess of the servants was down to the hijinks of the masters. But back to the story.

Nanna — There was one man who, knowin what I was all about, said to himself: 'I'll get what I want from her without payin.' So he came to my house all sweetness and light, entertained and flattered me and took care of my every whim; if I dropped somethin he'd pick it up and give it a kiss, then hand it to me with an elegant bow... Jaysus, I'm tellin ya. Then one day he suddenly says: 'I'd ask a favour from ye, my mistress. Then I'll die happy.' So I says to him: 'Ask and it shall be done.' 'I beg you,' he says, 'to come and sleep at mine tonight. I want my lady to have a little room I have prepared. I swear it will please you.' 'Alright,' I says, 'as you please', but only after I'd eaten, for I was having dinner with a friend. He was chuffed with this, for then he could brag he hadn't even had to buy me dinner. So that night I went and slept with him; but when we were done I stayed awake, and when I heard him snorin, put on his shirt in exchange for my blouse, for I'd already figured out which of his jewellery I wanted, and when my maidservant arrived I left the room, and gathered up all the linen that was out for washin, put the whole lot on the head of my maidservant and we scarpered home with the lot. What he had to say upon wakin, you can imagine.

Antonia — He had it comin.

Nanna — When he got up and saw my blouse, at first he thought I'd put his on by mistake, but when he realised everything was gone, he took me to court. They told the cheapo to take himself off. So it was me had the last laugh.

Antonia — So much the worse for him.

Nanna — Listen to this. I had a certain lover, a merchant, a good person who not only loved me but adored me and took care of me well, and I was by no means taken with him but I gave him an auld tug now and again. Sometimes you hear someone say: 'Such-and-such a whore is just dyin for your man there…'—Nonsense! It's bullshit. Now and again we have our heads turned by one big prick or another, and we want it ten ways from Sunday, but these follies last only as long as the winter sun. It's impossible for a woman who gives herself to everyone to fall in love with anyone.

Antonia — I know it well.

Nanna — Now this merchant was sleepin with me at his leisure. So to boost my reputation and really get him burnin for it, I made him crazy

jealous, while he kept on yappin that he wasn't in the least besotted
with me.

Antonia — How'd you do it?

Nanna — I sent out my porter—who was a rogue through and
through—to buy two pairs of partridges and a pheasant for dinner.
Later the porter came and knocked on the door while I was havin
dinner with the merchant, and when the maid answered he came in
with a: 'Good evening, m'lady—the Ambassador of Spain begs that
you come and enjoy this game with him when it's convenient to you.
He has something he'd like to share with you.' I snorted and said: 'The
who now? Who cares about this fellow? Take it away, I don't want it. And
don't bother me about this ambassador—can't you see I'm engaged?'
I turned to the daft merchant and gave him a little peck, then told the
porter to scoot. 'Why don't you take it, woman?' the merchant said.
'Take everything you can.' He shouted after the porter. 'She'll enjoy
them for the ambassador's sake,' he said and laughed. But after the
porter had left he was distracted, and I shook him and said: 'What's on
your mind? I haven't a moment even for the Emperor, never mind this
ambassador. I've more esteem for your boots than a million ducats.'
He showered me with kisses and went away to take care of business.
After, I ordered my heavies to come over to the house at nine, which is
when we usually had supper. They rustled up some daft little boy and
informed him of our plan, and at the appointed time had him come to
the house and knock on the door while we were eatin. When the boy
came inside he announced: 'Madam, my master the Lord Ambassador
has come to pay worship to your highness.' I replied: 'The Ambassador
will forgive me, since I am beholden to my master here,' and I put my
hand on my merchant's shoulder. The boy went out, hung around a
little, then came back. When we refused to open the door to him, he
shouted: 'Madam, if you don't open the door to my master he'll break
it down!' I went to the window and shouted: 'Your master can kill me,
throw me to the ground, and ruin me as he wishes, but I love only one

man and I'll die for him if needs be.' At this the thugs came bangin on the door, five or six of them but they sounded like a thousand; one of them in a huge voice bellowed: 'You whore, you'll regret this, and we'll murder that cuck who's under your thumb... by God, we'll wipe the floor with him!' 'Do what you will,' I shouted, 'but don't let on like you're a lord when you act like a dog!' To stop me shoutin more, the sap of a merchant tugged at my robe. 'Don't say another word or you'll have me cut to pieces by the Spaniards!' He pulled me inside, his head turned with all the words I'd said about him, with more gratitude than the prisoners they let out for the harvest festival. The next mornin he sent out for a gift for me, comin back with a satin robe. And he was so scared of the 'Spaniards' that you wouldnt've caught him out on the streets after the *Ave Maria* had been sung, not if you offered him a king's ransom. He was terrified of the Ambassador's sword. He said to me: 'My God, you know how to deal with these ambassadors!'

Antonia — Ambassadors?

Nanna — Because I made out I'd left nine of them in the lurch under the royal stairs, making them wait for me til dawn. I told him one night while he was sleepin with me that there was an ambassador out in the courtyard playin with himself, dreamin of me. Oh, that made him happy. And to ensure I'd never be seduced by the ambassadors, he ramped up the gifts, sayin: 'She's mine, and that's enough for me!'

Antonia — Ah, what a beautiful trick.

Nanna — Now *here's* a beautiful one... I often slept with a certain captain, who whenever anyone said to him, 'Watch out for that woman', he'd go into such a sulk and say: 'I mighta played around when I was with the guards in Siena and Genoa, but I don't give a raw cent to whores, not one!' Well, one day I noticed ten scudi in his purse, which I could've straight swiped on him that night, but I got it out of him in another way. As he was lyin in my bed, wrecked from the hammerin he'd just given me, I made out like I'd fallen for another man. When he went into a total tizzy, I went up to him, gave him two little tugs on his beard, sat down in his lap and said: 'Who is your sweet little whore?' I parted his thighs with my knee and rubbed my arse against his baby maker, and kissed him gently on the face until he got so wound up he said: 'It's you, my angel', and he fell silent with a sigh which I felt on my face like a breeze, and I caressed him so nicely he relaxed and came back to himself. And as I was whisperin to him, 'I wish we could sleep together tonight', someone who'd been put up to it rapped the door, and the maid, goin to the window, came back and said: 'Madam, the haberdasher is here.' 'Tell him to come up,' I said. When he came up he asked me for ten scudi I owed him for some curtains, beggin me to be quick about it as he was busy. So I says to the maid: 'Take this key and open the chest and give him ten scudi.' She went off to open it, leavin me to work my magic with the man who thought he was above all ruse. He was already enchanted, so when the artisan hurried me and I scolded the maid: 'Hurry up you daftie!', hearing her grumble I went to see what she was up to with the chest. Well, she couldn't open it, and since even the tailor who'd come for the money was a put-up, so the key was also a ruse, since it wasn't made for that lock. I let on she'd broken it and gave her a smart about the head. Then I told her to break it open, but there was no hammer to be found. Then I turned to the captain and said: 'Please sir, if you have ten scudi, give it to him. I'll break this chest open if I have to, but I swear you'll get your money back.'

Antonia — Quite the polite lady, you are, when it comes to the important matters, ha ha!

Nanna — He pulled out his purse and threw down the money. 'Take them, maestro, and go with God.' I gave the chest a good kick like I wanted to break it. 'Send out for a locksmith later. There's no hurry,' he said offhandedly, talkin down to me, as if now I was in his debt.

Antonia — What an arse.

Nanna — When I left off with the kickin I threw myself into bed with him, but I'd no intention of going the whole way. That's why, no sooner was I in his arms than again there was a hammerin on the door. I went to jump up and he pulled at me, beggin me to leave it. I looked outside and saw it was a gentleman in a hat and a cape sittin on his mule. He gave his mule a little slap on the rump and bade me come down. I said alright, takin the cape from my manservant—cause I was dressed up like a boy, as I usually was—and went off with him. So my beater of whores, the merchant, slashed up one of my portraits and set fire to my chamber in revenge, then left, like a gambler of ill-repute skulking out of the game. He even busted open the chest to get his money back. My maid shouted out the window: 'Thieves! Thieves!', by which time a whole crowd had come runnin. Havin busted open the chest, he found it full of ointments and oils, and he was chased out of there. I swear, Antonia, by tellin you all these things I feel like a sinner who wants to confess, but when she finds herself at the friar's feet, she can't even remember half of what she did.

Antonia — Tell me what you remember. Like that I'll be able to judge what you've forgotten.

Nanna — So I will. There was a certain knucklehead who had a vineyard, all he owned in the world but which had earned him about a hundred ducats... so he got it in his head he wanted me for a wife. He mentioned this to my hairdresser who passed it onto me. Well, when I heard about the cash, I started dropping little hints by way of the hairdresser, and soon he got so sure he could throw the noose around me he showed up at my house. I indulged him in all sorts of little caresses, and in only a month he'd furnished the whole house: beds, kitchen, the lot, and I only let him have a dip at me once or twice, no more. After that, I started a barney with him over some nonsense and called him a horse's ass, a scoundrel, rascal, miser, galoot, ignoramus... then slammed the door in his face. After realisin what had happened, the wretch turned monk, and I was happy.

Antonia — Happy?

Nanna — The more a whore can boast of havin ruined a man or driven him mad, the more her value increases.

Antonia — Then she's the envy of all.

Nanna — I can't tell ya how much silver I've made by puttin one over this man or that. Men would come to dine at my house, and after dinner the cards would come out. 'Come on,' I'd say, 'let's play for two julios' worth of candy. The man with the King of Cups pays.' And after they'd lost and paid for the candy, well, the cards were on the table and that was it. They couldn't stop playin any more than a whore can stop screwin. So they played. Two of my plants would come in then and sit down, men who looked like idiots, and let themselves get taken for a bit. Soon they were cleanin up, and it was me indicatin to them by secret sign what hands the others were holdin.

Antonia — Now that's a saucy hoax.

Nanna — For two ducats I informed this one fellow how his mortal enemy was coming to my house one day before sunrise. When the day came, the man was layin in wait. He hacked the fellow to pieces.

Antonia — What beastliness, Nanna. But why was he comin before sunrise?

Nanna — Because that was just the time another man was leavin. Antonia, do you think if I was sleepin with one man, he was the only one stirrin the pot? A thousand times I rolled out from beside some merchant, sayin I had bellyache or somethin, then ran downstairs to some fella who was hidin in the cellar. Or I'd blame the heat and get up to go pace the hall for a bit, stoppin to lean out the window to talk with the moon and stars, and there'd be a fella there to take me from behind, sometimes two of em for a laugh.

Antonia — But what's gone, you're not gettin back.

Nanna — No doubt about it. Now get this one. After I'd drained ten or twelve of my tricks and they couldn't provide for me anymore, I decided to do away with em for good.

Antonia — And how'd you do that?

Nanna — I used to give apples and fennel to two physician friends of mine, men I could trust. But one day I said to them: 'I want to pretend to be ill, so my boys will flock to the house to take care of me. You,' I said to the doctor, 'will order me to bed and send for medicines, which you,' I indicated my apothecary friend, 'will record in your book and send my way.'

Antonia — I think I get ya—like this you skimmed all the money your lovers were givin the doctor and the apothecary.

Nanna — You're quick. Anyway, I could hardly keep from laughin at dinner that night when I faked a swoon and fell at the foot of the table. My mother, who knew the score, put on a look of terror as she helped carry me to the bed. She was practically in mourning. I came to, sighed, and cried: 'O my poor heart!' And they tripped over themselves, shoutin, 'It's nothing!', 'It's just the evil vapours', and as I came around I told em I was well but then fainted again in anguish, sendin two of them runnin for the doctor. He came and took my pulse and roused me with rosy vinegars, sayin: 'Her heart still beats!' Half the lovers followed my mother out of the room, afraid she was gonna throw herself out the window, the others gathered around the doctor who was writin the prescription. When he finished one of them took it in person to the apothecary and came back laden with powders and ampoules. After the doctor had instructed them all, he left, and my mother had great trouble chasin them from the house. When mornin came they all returned along with the doctor, and he, hearin of the awful night I'd had, ordered they should find twenty-five ducats to pay for a certain tonic. One of the dupes gave the money immediately to my ma, who swiftly deposited it into our stash. In short, what with all the rhubarb tonics, syrups, cordials, enemas, juleps and doctor's fees, not to mention the wood and the candles, we were showered with silver.

Antonia — Didn't you get fed up layin in bed?

Nanna — I would've, if I'd been alone. But one night the doctor would massage my shoulders, and the next the apothecary would give me a good rub down, and when I was better, I was utterly spoiled on capons and good wine. Nearly every cellar in the city was ransacked to take care of me.

Antonia — Ha ha ha!

Nanna — So this merchant that I told you about, made it known, without sayin it in so many words, that he wanted to have a son with me. I began to put it on, pretendin to fall into a depression, and from mornin to evenin I was antsy and snappy. Every other mouthful of food I'd spit it out and cry, 'What disgusting thing is this?' and make like I was about to throw up. All the while this fellow was sayin quietly to himself: 'Oh, God willing!' I ate like a hog when he wasn't around, and when he was I made like I wasn't hungry and wouldn't touch a crumb, and after feigning every kind of cramp, mornin sickness, kidney ailment, and lettin on like I'd missed my period, I let him know through my mother that I was pregnant. My doctor confirmed it. So this shit-for-brains, happy as you like, went about appointing godmother and godfather, started stockpiling food and diapers, and even took on a wet-nurse. Not a little bird was put up for sale, nor a fruit or flower that he didn't snatch up for me in case the baby came to some detriment. He couldn't even stand for me to bring my hands to my mouth and instead would feed me himself, and he was there at my side whenever I wanted to get up or sit down. And I laughed to see how much he cried after I told him: 'If I die giving birth, take care of our son for me.' I even made a will which made him heir of all my possessions. He went around showin it off to everyone he met, sayin to them: 'Read it... read it and tell me I'm wrong to worship this woman.' One day, after this had gone on for some time, I threw myself to the floor in a very dramatic fashion. I made on like I was really hurt, and had the maidservant bring in a basin of lukewarm water that had a stillborn lamb in it—you would've swore it was a human baby. When he saw it, the tears fell; he began wailin and gnashin, and when my mother told him it was a boy, and that it looked like him, he spent I-dunno-how-many ducats having the child buried. We made him dress up in black for the funeral, and boy did he despair because the baby hadn't been baptised.

Antonia — Who was Pippa's father?

Nanna — I swear to God, he was a marquis. But for all the world I can't mention his name. Please let's talk about somethin else.

Antonia — As you like.

Nanna — I had a notion to take up the lute, not because I felt like it, but for the show of delighting in the Arts. Truth is, the virtues of whores are only decoration for ensnaring fools, and they cost more than they're worth. If you ever encounter a whore that can sing or read, run a mile. Barefoot if you have to.

Antonia — Everything in this world is a deception.

Nanna — Above all else, I had a knack at turnin everything to my advantage. I could 'reap the deacon's flowerbeds', as Margutte says. There wasn't a one slept with me I didn't strip of somethin. Believe me, the shirt, the cap, the shoe or hat, or sword or cape that was left in my house was never again seen. There's a buyer for everything, and anything can be turned to silver. Because of this, I was pally with the water-carriers, the wood-sellers, the oil merchants, those who sold doughnuts, soap, milk, chestnuts, even the shoe-shiners and the match vendors. They were all my friends, and would compete to see who could send the most customers my way.

Antonia — Why were they doin that?

Nanna — Because I'd go to the window for any old excuse, and whoever wanted to bed me was forced to spend a julio or a drachma with the merchants. For example, the maid might pop her head in the door and say, 'The pillowcases are threadbare. You need more cloth.' I'd give whatever man was at hand a kiss and say: 'Give her a julio.' And the one who didn't would be marked as a filthy miser. After the maid, my mother would show up, hands full of linen: 'Don't let this pass you by... you'll never see such a bargain again.' So I'd give two kisses to another fella, and soon the linen was taken care of. Once that little party was over, another boyo would happen along, and I'd butter him up with kisses and caresses til he was simmering, and stewed just the right way he'd soon be sendin me silk bedsheets or a painting, and any other thing of beauty I had a fancy for. In return for this gift I promised him he could come and sleep with me, so when the night came and he sent me a terrific dinner, then showed up to enjoy it with me, I'd tell him to take a walk and return in a little bit, and when he came back, the servant would say, 'Just a little while more.' He'd wait, knock again, and get no answer. Then he'd shout: 'You whore! Pig! I swear by the body of the Immaculate Mother, you'll pay for this!' All while I dined and laughed with another at his expense.

Antonia — How did he forgive you afterwards?

Nanna — Usually he'd stew for a couple of days until he could no longer bite his lip, then he'd send a servant to say he wanted a word. 'Just a word?' I'd say. When I eventually opened the door to him, he'd be huffin and puffin. 'I never expected this from you,' he'd say. 'My love,' I'd tell him, 'believe me or don't, I like, love nor cherish any man but you, and if you knew why I took leave of you that night, you would praise me. If I can't rely on you, who can I rely on?' And I rolled out any old excuse about bein at the house of some lawyer or prosecutor regarding a quarrel, then I'd throw my arms around his neck and let him stick his flute in my flute case. And all the while I was rippin out his heart and polluting his soul, so that the claws were in him and he couldn't tear himself away. Yes, he was singin my praises again by the time I was done.

Antonia — You should've made yourself a singing teacher.

Nanna — Oh, by grace, I should have.

Antonia — And by your consummate skill.

Nanna — You're too kind. But wait til you hear how I almost made myself filthy rich. There was an old gentleman who was dyin for it and wanted me to go with him to one of his estates for two months. So I started puttin it about that I wanted to marry the Lord and made a deal with a Jew for all my possessions. God, this put my lovers through the wringer. Once I had the money, I put it all in a bank without anyone's knowledge. Then I went off with this gentleman.

Antonia — Why did you sell your possessions?

Nanna — So I could replace the lot after! Anyway, when I came back, they all rushed to buy new stuff for me.

Antonia — Oh, what a witch you are. Such mischief you sowed among them.

Nanna — I don't deny, a whore uses every wile at her disposal to blind the dupes. You won't believe me, but if I wanted, I could make them eat my shit, even drink my period. There was one girl—I won't name her—who to make her lover chase her all the more, made him eat the crusty clap sores on her pussy. And she had plenty.

Antonia — Aw, that's absolutely foul.

Nanna — Tis. But listen to this. Using a candle made from the body fat of a man burned alive at the stake, I once warmed up a little pot of my own bodily expulsions and made a man drink it. But I swear, these enchantments they have like using the rope a man was hanged with or a dead man's fingernails, or diabolical incantations, are nothing compared to the greatest devilry, that I'd tell you of if it weren't forbidden to mention.

Antonia — Ah. Your conscience is clean, then.

Nanna — Not to seem hypocritical, but I swear, a fat peachy arse can do more than all the philosophers, astrologers, alchemists and necromancers combined. I've sampled more herbs than you can grow in two whole meadows, and paid for as many incantations as a word-peddler can spout, but I could never thaw the heart of this certain man—I can't tell you his name—but with a single shake of my arse I made such a beast of him that all the whores were dumbstruck, and these are women that have seen everything.

Antonia — Ah Nanna, you know all about enchantment.

Nanna — The finest enchantment is in the slit between the thighs, which has the power to extract silver from shinbones.

Antonia — Better for a woman to have an arse than money then. She has more power.

Nanna — More power for sure. But let's follow this train of thought and note down this particular cunning, which is very important. I had one lover who'd fly off the handle at the littlest thing. In a single moment somethin would rattle his cage and set him off, at which he'd curse me to hell, and the next minute when his fury had subsided, he'd throw himself at my feet with his hands clasped in prayer and beg forgiveness. His penance was his purse; he paid in coin. One day when he was falling out of favour, I drove him to absolute despair by gettin out of the bed and goin downstairs to give myself to one of his rivals, and he got so livid he gave me a beating. And after, thinkin I'd never listen to his shit again, he gave me a full half of his purse to calm me.

Antonia — You're like one of those men who swears not to attack his enemy. Then, when his guard is down, he goads him into having a shot at him so as to give him an excuse to go on the assault.

Nanna — That's exactly what I was, ha ha! I almost piss my knickers when I think of the preacher who dreamt up only seven deadly sins to cover every sinner in the world—even the most despondent whore in the world can drum up a hundred. How many sins must a woman have who must strip a thousand churches to cover her own altar? Listen to me, Antonia: gluttony, wrath, pride, envy, sloth and avarice were born the day the whore was born; if you want to know how a whore feeds herself, think about those she feeds on; and if you want to know how wrathful a whore is in her rage, think about the mother and father of all the saints. Know this: if a whore could send the whole world into the pits of hell, they'd do it in less time than it took the Creator to create it.

Antonia — A bad business.

Nanna — The pride of a whore is greater than that of a villain; a whore's envy devours itself, just like syphilis eats at those who carry it in their bones.

Antonia — Dear God, don't remind me. I caught it once, and I've no idea where from.

Nanna — Forgive me for bringin it up. I forgot it almost killed you. Anyway, the sloth of a whore is deeper than that of a rake who rots away in a tiny shack without a penny to his name. The avarice of a whore is like a stingy banker who's driven by greed to steal tiny morsels and squirrel them away with all the other scraps.

Antonia — And what about the lust of a whore?

Nanna — Antonia, she who always drinks is never too thirsty, and seldom hungry she who's always at the table. And if at any time they come across a big ol' piddler, they go at it with the appetite of a pregnant woman for a fruit salad. I swear by the good fortune I wish for Pippa, that lust is the least of our problems, because we're always thinkin up ways of cuttin out men's hearts.

Antonia — I swear you've convinced me.

Nanna — You may well believe me, but now let me gift you a thousand little trickeries in a single breath.

Antonia — Tell me.

Nanna — There were three fellas among all the men who loved me, an artist and two other suitors, and I swear they were like dogs and cats when they were around each other, and when one thought the other two were away he would lurk about like a cretin. One day the painter came to my door at an ungodly hour, nearly beatin it down, and no sooner was he up the stairs and sittin next to me but one of the others was at the door too. Knowing who it was, I told the painter to stay put and went down to see the other man, who came in shoutin: 'By the Devil, if I get my hands on that bloody painter...' But the painter, upstairs, couldn't hear what was goin on. And while he was rattlin on, the third one starts clappin on the door. So I hid the fellow that hated the painter and went to the door, and this other fella comes in in a tizzy. 'I thought I'd find you here with those other two wretches. By God, if they were here, they'd be missin an ear right now.' And don't think for an instant that because he talked the talk he'd be ready to give a man a good kick in the arse. In fact, the opposite, because when the painter heard him (not knowin of the second), and the second heard him (not knowin the painter was upstairs), they both leapt out at the same time, ready to ram the third suitor's words down his throat. Seein both of em, he shrunk and ran to the head of the stairs, and tumbled all the way to the bottom, and the other two, not missin an opportunity, heaped on top of him. Such a brawl ensued between these three men that a crowd gathered outside the door, but not for love of tryin could they get the door open to tear them off each other. As the crowd outside were raisin a furore, a governor happened to pass by, and havin the door of the house torn down, had the three men dragged bloody and beaten to prison, and they'd never had gotten out if they hadn't come to some sort of agreement.

Antonia — What a beautiful ending.

Nanna — It's such a good story I used to tell it to all the out-of-towners. I almost had a song written about it by Gianmaria the Jew, but I didn't want to seem boastful.

Antonia — God will reward you in heaven.

Nanna — He better. But if this story made everyone laugh, the one I'll tell you now shocked them. When I was at the height of my renown due to being such a hot ticket, I took a notion to get myself cloistered at the Campo Santo.

Antonia — Why not St. Peter's or St. John's?

Nanna — Because I wanted to move others to greater pity by placing myself among the bones of so many dead.

Antonia — An honourable plan.

Nanna — To live up to the honour, I began to live a holy life.

Antonia — Before you tell me more, tell me why you wanted to get yourself walled up.

Nanna — Why? To get away from all my lovers. And do it at their expense.

Antonia — Of course you did.

Nanna — I began to change my life. First thing I did was strip the bedroom: the bed, the table, the whole lot, then I got rid of my necklaces, rings, hats, shoes and put on a horsehair dress and gave to fasting every day, though I managed to eat plenty on the sly. I stopped talkin, but not all the time, and I gave my lovers only a little taste. Day after day I weaned them off me, and soon they began to despair. Once word of my plan to be cloistered had spread all over, I took everything valuable from the house and put it away somewhere safe, and I began to hand out rags to the needy, just for God's grace. And when the time approached, I called all my lovers—it'd been better for them if they'd lost me outright and not bit by bit—and told them to sit down. After we'd been sittin there for some time, turnin over a few words in my head which I'd been dreamin up, I let a few tears drop onto my pale cheeks and said: 'Brothers, fathers, sons... he who doesn't think of the soul, either doesn't have one or doesn't cherish it. But I hold mine dear—it was converted by a preacher and by the legend of St. Chiepina, and also frightened by the pictures of hell that I've seen painted, and I've resolved not to end up in the hellfire. Since my sins are smaller than God's mercy, my brothers, my sons, I want to wall up my filthy flesh and imprison this wretched existence!' Hearin this, the sobs rattled in their throats, like they do in those of the devout, who can't hold back their fervour when listening to the friar tell of the Passion. Then I said: 'No more luxuries, no more high fashion, no more trickery—my lavish room shall become naked, my bed shall be a handful of straw threwn on a pallet, rainwater my drink and the grace of God my sustenance. And my golden gown I shall shed for this...' And at that I pulled from under the seat the roughest type of hairshirt. Good God, if you remember the weepin that the people break into when they unveil the holy cross at the Coliseum, this is the display my lovers fell into, all choked with sorrow and weak with tears. When I said, 'Brothers, I ask your forgiveness,' they raised a roar like the sack

of Rome, God save us. One of them threw himself at my feet, and not
bein able to turn me with his pleading words, he got up and smacked
his head twenty times into the wall.

Antonia — Aw. A shame.

Nanna — Now came the mornin I was to enter the cloister, and
you'd have sworn all Rome was in the church of Campo Santo. If
you gathered together everyone that gathers at a Jewish baptism
you wouldn't come close to the people there, and I'm tellin ya, not
a convict on the day of his execution nor a soldier readying for battle
suffered more than my lovers did. But I don't wanna beat around the
bush; as all there lamented, I was walled up. One man cried, 'God has
filled her heart!', another: 'Just look at the example she's setting for
the other whores.' Yet someone else said: 'Who'd have believed it!'
Some were amazed, some laughed, saying: 'If she makes it to the end
of the month, you can crucify me!' It was heartbreaking and a hoot
to see my paramours all day long in the church, all wrangling to get a
word with me. The Pharisees did not watch over the Holy Sepulchre
as well as those fellows watched over me. And soon I gave ear to the
prayers they were sendin up from mornin to night, askin that I might
come out. 'A woman can save her soul from anyplace', they implored,
over and over. To cut a long story short, they talked me into it, and in
the end they broke down the walls of the place the way they break the
Jubilee gate after the Pope has felled the first brick. So they furnished
a whole house for me and I became even more brazen than before, and
all of Rome was in stitches. The ones who had predicted my downfall
hollered out to each other: 'Didn't I tell ya!'

Antonia — I don't know how a woman could think up what you did.

Nanna — Whores are not women, they are whores. And that's how
I thought up and did what I did. Don't take lightly the wisdom we
owe to the ants and the squirrels, who amass in summer so they may
be stocked in winter. Antonia, sister, know that a whore always has
a thorn in her heart that disturbs her peace of mind; it's the fear of

endin up a beggar on the church steps like you talked about before. But for every one like myself who knows how to till her field, there are a thousand who die in the poorhouse. Master Andrea used to say that whores and tricks can be weighed on the same scale; most of them resemble old coins rather than gold. And that thorn, that not only pierces the heart but also the soul, what does that do but make the whore think of old age? So she goes to the poorhouse and picks out the fairest girl there and takes her home and raises her as her own, and as the child comes of age as the old whore's gettin over the hill, she'll give her the loveliest name and change it from day to day, so that today she's Giulia and tomorrow Laura, the next day Lucretia and the day after that Cassandra, or Portia or Virginia or Prudence or Cornelia, and then she'll put her out on the street. For every one child who has a real mother, as I am to Pippa, there are a thousand lifted from the hospital. Because there's no knowin who the father of a whore's child is—though of course we always claim they're the daughters of lords and monsignors. But there are so many seeds scattered in our gardens that it's impossible to say who planted it there. It's a fool of a whore who boasts she knows the origin of a single stalk in a field with twenty different strains of wheat.

Antonia — No doubt about it.

Nanna — God help the poor bastard who's discussed by a whore and her mother behind closed doors. For if they're gettin on in years, they'll be out to fleece him. Such treacheries and thievery these women will teach their daughters! They'll take care of him who feeds them well, and so they always embroil themselves with younger men—this is the habit of old women on their last legs.

Antonia — It's as you say, still to this day.

Nanna — A fencing teacher does not teach so many nasty pricks and stabs as that old mother teaches. She'll tell her: 'When this fella shows up, tell him such-and-such a thing, and ask him this and leave him like that, and touch him in this manner and be angry when he says this... don't piss him off too much and don't be too sweet with him, and while you're teasin him go look out the window pensively, make him promises as it suits you, and grab whatever rings or necklaces you can. The worst that can happen is he demands it back.'

Antonia — I can almost believe it.

Nanna — Believe me.

Antonia — Have you done all these dirty tricks?

Nanna — One woman who spreads her legs is just like the next; while I lived as a whore I was a whore. I did nothin a whore didn't do... I wouldnt've been a whore if I didn't have the lusts of a whore. If there was ever a woman who deserved the name 'whore', it was Nanna; I excelled at not lookin a day over twenty-five. It'd be easier to count the fireflies in ten different countries than guess the true age of a whore; today she tells you 'I'm twenty!', and six years later will swear she's only nineteen. But let's move on to more important things. Can you guess how many poor unfortunates I've cut down and left for dead in my day?

Antonia — I'll have a guess after your last day.

Nanna — Oh, Jesus... by the time that day comes I'll have paid so many indulgences and completed so many stations of the cross that I'll have bought my soul a little mercy, and my soul'll not be the least of them in the afterlife just as my body was not the least in this world. Mother of God, no—I'll not be the last, even if I've taken great pleasure in seein men kill each other over me. I did it out of vanity, for it seemed a just flattery of my beauty to hear swords clashing night after night on my account. God help the man who looked at me the wrong way, because he had the sword hangin over him.

Antonia — Evil is evil, and good is good.

Nanna — All things in their proper place. I've done evil and I've repented. But how can I tell you the flair I had for bringin the hammer down upon a lover? Antonia, sometimes I had ten of em in the house together, and I dished out kisses and caresses and sweet words with so much grace they all thought they were in heaven. Then one day a new bird flies into my coop all dressed up in the finest fashion and decked to the nines, and I welcome the gift horse inside, leaving my lovers on the recliner and takin the new beau to my chamber. This would cause those left outside in the hall to wither, like almonds falling from the autumn tree. I'd hear them sigh in silence, and they gathered together for warmth like birds in a nest. After this they'd begin to panic, bite at their fingernails and bring their fists down upon the table, scratch their heads in silent confusion and hum distractedly to soothe their anger. Then they'd make their way down the stairs, announcing their exit loudly, hopin I'd call them back, and doin a lap outside they'd come back to find the door locked. That was a spiteful welcome.

Antonia — Ancroia was not so cruel as you.

Nanna — Don't pity these cretins.

Antonia — I do.

Nanna — Eh, if that's the way you want to be. So long as you hear me.

Antonia — I'm listenin, believe me.

Nanna — You should've seen me, caught up in the pleasure of being taken by a man, and all of a sudden burstin into tears for no reason. And when he'd say, 'Why are you crying?', I'd sob and sigh and weep and sputter: 'I'm so torn—you don't appreciate me. It's my bad luck that I can do nothing about it.' Another time, when a fellow was leavin me for two hours, I wept and said to him: 'Where are you going? To one of your other whores who'll treat you as you deserve?' And the chump would feel all big-headed that he'd made a woman suffer for him. I also wept when one showed up who hadn't seen me in a couple of days, to make him believe I was overjoyed to see him again.

Antonia — You had tears comin out your ears.

Nanna — I was like a spring that could gush forth at will; but I never wept but with one eye.

Antonia — Wept with one eye?

Nanna — Whores weep with one eye. Wives with two, nuns with four.

Antonia — That's a wisdom worth knowin.

Nanna — It certainly is. Whores cry with one eye and laugh with the other.

Antonia — This is even more beautiful. Explain what you mean.

Nanna — Don't you know, you poor thing, that we whores always have laughter in one eye and in the other weeping? For every little thing we laugh at, there's some other little thing to make us weep. Our eyes are like a clouded sun, which now shoots forth bright rays, only to hide it a second later. From laughter, tears. And when it came to tears and laughter, I could turn it on better than any Spanish whore. With these two skills, I put more men to the knife than those who die in pallets in cold cells. There are no better tools in a whore's arsenal than laughter and weeping; but they must be used at the right time, for if the opportunity slips you by, their effect is nil; like damask roses, they must be picked at dawn or they lose their scent.

Antonia — Every day's a school day.

Nanna — After the laughter and the fake tears come their sister—the lies. And I enjoy these more than a fat farmer enjoys a pancake. No exaggeration, I've told more lies than the Gospels tell truths. These lies were built so robustly with the lime of my word and my oaths that others accepted them without fail. I invented the most contemptible stories in the world, about my connections and my estates, and my accomplishments... I came up with some very tall tales indeed, and turned em all to my advantage. In a small book I kept a record of the name of all my conquests, and like that I divvied out the nights of the week between them, posting the name of the man who'd sleep with me that night. Oh, I was organised. If you've seen those boards in the sacristy that post the names of the priests who say mass, you'll know somethin of my system.

Antonia — I've seen those lists of the priests. Yours must have been very methodical indeed.

Nanna — No woman could match me for discipline.

Antonia — But what does the book of names have to do with the lies you were tellin?

Nanna — It has to do with these dafties who thought they had it made after seein their name on the door which told them their night with me, but it didn't always tell the truth. In fact, it often changed, just like it happens that the church changes who's sayin the mass.

Antonia — Ah. Now I see the connection.

Nanna — Now get a load of this, and by your honour, keep it to yourself. So I once decided to filch this expensive golden chain from one fellow who was dyin to sleep with me, a chain he'd borrowed from some gentleman who'd stripped it from his wife. And the first day he hung it around my neck was the day the Pope grants dowries to many poor young girls in the Church of the Minerva.

Antonia — The day of the Annunciation?

Nanna — Exactly. I put it around my neck on that very day, but it wasn't there for long.

Antonia — Why?

Nanna — Because it was when I was in the church and saw the crowds I decided to pinch it. To set up the rip-off, I took the necklace off and slipped it to a friend who was very discreet. Then I pushed my way into the throng and let out a shriek like those who have their teeth yanked out by some quack doctor in the Campo di Fiore. When everyone spun around to see what was goin on, here was Nanna, screamin: 'My chain, my chain! Thief! Rogue!' and I let the tears stream down my face. The whole church was in uproar, upset by this screechin of mine, and the report made it all the way to the sheriff, who dragged some poor wretch to the Torre di Nona. He was almost hanged on the spot.

Antonia — God, don't tell me any more.

Nanna —Oh, you'll listen girl.

Antonia — I want to hear what the man who lent it to you had to say.

Nanna — I came out of church weepin and wringin my hands, and when I got home I locked myself in my room and said to the nursemaid: 'Don't let anyone disturb me!' So this fellow shows up and wants to talk to me, but when there's no answer he beats on the door and shouts: 'Nanna? Nanna!? Open up, open up I say... what are you getting in such a state about?' Lettin on I was in despair, I said: 'I'm such a poor, unlucky wretch. I'm going to enter in the convent, I want to drown myself, I want to be a hermit!' I got up from the bed where I lay, and without openin the door I shouted to the maid: 'Go and find me a Jew. I want to sell everything I own. I'll pay for the chain with the money.' And when he saw my maid headin out to do my bidding, my lover pounded on the door shoutin: 'Open the door to me!' So I opened up. 'I've had it, I'm done for!' I said. And he: 'Don't worry, you haven't lost everything. I'm gonna do what I can to help.' 'No, no,' I said, 'give me two months and I'll take care of it.' 'Stop now, you poor thing!' he said, and takin me to bed I showed him such a sweet time that there wasn't another word said about the chain.

Antonia — Many things came in and out of that door of yours, Nanna.

Nanna — So there was this wrinkled old rake of a thing took a likin to me, and I took a shine to his wallet. And since he could indulge his pleasures just as any toothless sot can enjoy a hard auld crust of bread, he took great joy in touchin me up, kissin me, and suckin on my tits, but not for love nor money could he raise the pole, not even with all the truffles or artichokes in the world. Even if he got it to poke the head up it quickly fell back down, like the lamp that has just a trickle of oil in it and sputters then dies. I could pull at it and shake it all I wanted, or stick a finger up his toothole or fondle his balls—nah, nothin did the job. Well, I played many a daft trick on the old fool. Once I ordered a feast for all my lovers that he had to stump up for, and nicked four of the silver plates he'd ordered for the dinner. When he grumbled about it, I jumped into his lap and cried, 'Oh daddy, don't be mad— you know it'll give you a gippy stomach. Why don't you take all my dresses, and you can pay for them with that.' That shut him up, for I gave him so many 'daddys' and 'papis' that I turned his heart. He paid for the dishes out of his own pocket and swore he'd never borrow anything from anyone again, ever.

Antonia — Oh, you're sly as a fox.

Nanna — In the beginning of an affair I was so sweet and affectionate that the man would sing my praises to the high heavens, but it wasn't long before the manna turned sour; and if in the beginning I showed distaste for bad behaviour, then in the middle and the end of an affair I showed only a dislike of the good. In the manner of any whore of worth I took delight in causin scandal, startin a ruckus, breakin up friendships, stirrin animosity, listenin to the worst villainy and puttin men at each other's throats. I was always name-dropping princes and sittin in judgement on Turks, the Emperor, the King, the riches of the Duke of Milan, the future Pope. I asserted that the stars were as big as the pineapple on top of St. Peter's and no bigger, that the moon was the bastard sister of the sun; from dukes to duchesses I moseyed, first exalting them then speaking as if I used them for a doormat; I had all the airs of an empress, which, by the way, would hardly be befitting her, and in any case are all make-believe. I took inspiration from that noblewoman who carried a silk cushion around with her and made whoever spoke to her kneel on it.

Antonia — You mean the female Pope?

Nanna — The lady Pope—as they called her—did not put on so many graces as me. And she didn't even give herself such a title as whores carry. Some of us made ourselves the daughter of Duke Valentino, another the child of Cardinal Ascanio, and Madrema called herself 'Lucrezia Portia, Patrician of Rome', and imprinted her letters with a great big seal. And these titles made them no better women; they were still devoid of love, charity, pity... so much so that if St. Job or St. Anthony begged them for alms, they wouldn't hand over a penny.

Antonia — Nasty bitches!

Nanna — Believe me, better toss what you have into the river than give it to a whore. Soon as you give them anything, they despise you as much as they'd let on to respect you before, and the only good thing about em is their faith, which they cling to like gypsies or Indian monks. In short, whores have honey on their tongues but their hands hide a razor; you might see em butter each other up without shame, and the minute they turn their backs they spout such poison it'd frighten Desiderio and the priests who scared Death by laughin at him. They're backstabbers through and through, with no regard for anyone no matter what good they've done. You'll think she's smitten with one of her lovers she keeps as a favourite, and she'll flatter him countless times with 'Yes, your lordship!', and when he leaves before another comes in she'll pay him a thousand honours, but the minute he's down the stairs she'll spit bitterness and curse him worse than a traitor, so the new dupe thinks himself the apple of his mammy's eye.

Antonia — Why do they do that?

Nanna — Because a whore is no whore if she's not treacherous but with grace and privilege; a whore without a whore's traits is like macaroni without cheese.

Antonia — It must be a great relief to those men who've been ruined by whores to see them go up on the gallows. Like that woman in the poem, you know, the one that goes:

> *Madrema does not wish it, nor Lorenzina,*
>
> *or Laura, or Cecilia, or Beatrice;*
>
> *Let this be an example to you, this wretched tart.*

I know it by heart. I learned it thinkin it was by Master Andrea, then I found out that other fella did it who treats the great lords worse than this ill disease treats me; not perfume or unguents or medicines help at all. Ah, sweet patience.

Nanna — I don't know what else to tell you, more than I've already said. I'm thinkin. I swear, my brain's like a bag of old laundry. It's only fit for shellin peas. I'm all over the place. Wait now, listen to this. This young fella of around twenty-two came to Rome, he was noble and rich, a merchant. Great pickings for a whore. When he first arrived, he threw himself at me, and I pretended I was head over heels in love with him. And the more brazen he got, the more desperate I let on I was. I started sendin my maid four, five, six times a day beggin him to come and see me, and soon it got about that I was cooked like a goose, fit only for the priest to say the last rites. 'Finally that slut has been fitted up good and proper', folk went about sayin, 'and by who? By a young buck still with the taste of the wet nurse's tit in his mouth! He'll drive her to wit's end!' I kept mum, and let on like I was wastin away from love for him, not able to eat, not able to sleep, always pining in misery and callin upon him. They were takin bets as to how long it was til I'd be driven mad and end up on the streets, destroyed by his beautiful eyes. Well, the young fella got a few nights out of it, and a few dinners too, and went about boastin and showin off this cheap turquoise trinket I'd given him, and when he was with me I kept sayin: 'Don't worry about money—leave it to me. What's mine is yours. You have me, faithfully and completely.' Then he'd go saunterin down the Via dei Banchi and people would point at him and say, 'That's him!' Then one day this great squire came to visit while he was with me, and I told the young fella to hide in my closet and sent the maid down to let the squire in. He came in and sat himself down. Seein my new white linen bedsheets, he said: 'Who's going to break them in for you?' I replied, 'My lover will... I love him and adore him, he's my God and I his servant, and will be forever.' This got the young fella all puffed up when he heard it, you can be sure. When the squire left and he came out of the closet, his shirt was no longer touching his arse. He strutted about the house, surveying everything like he owned me, the servants and the whole household. But let's get to the 'Amen' of this Our Father... one day he wanted to fuck me in his favourite way over a chest. I got down on my knees, and just as he was about to make his Hail Mary I got up and stole into the bedroom where I had another man waitin, and locked myself in there. Well, the young stud wasn't used to this tomfoolery, so he grabbed his cape, cursin me out, and stormed off thinkin I'd chase after him like I was prone to. But when the peace pigeon didn't fly down as usual, the Devil came on him and he flew into a rage, and at the door he was told by the maid: 'My lady is busy.' Boy oh boy, he was like a rat dipped in hot oil. He staggered away from the house, his eyes wet and his legs tremblin like an old man's. I watched through the curtains, seeing the jealousy carved across his back as he walked away. God I laughed. He came back in the evenin and I opened the door to him. I had a whole host of fellows there that night, and we were all havin a jolly time of it. I didn't invite him to sit but he joined all the same, sittin quietly in the corner and not sayin a word. He sat there til the last of the others had left. As soon as we were alone he says to me: 'Where's all your love now? Your caresses? Your promises?' And I says: 'Brother, thanks to you I'm the laughing stock of all the whores in Rome. They take the piss out of me day and night because of my idiocy. And what cooks my goose most is my lovers don't want to give me anything anymore. They say, "Why should we pay for the bacon soup and get only croutons?" But if you want me to be to you what I was before, then do one thing for me...' At this his head shot up. He told me he'd raise heaven and earth if he had to. 'Just say the word,' he says. 'Right then—I want a new bed,' I says, 'and what with the skirting, the satin and the bedding, the whole thing'll cost about 190 ducats or thereabouts. And I want my friends to think you're willin to go in hock for me, so buy it on credit. When the time comes, I'll make the others pay for it, I swear to you.' 'Out of the question,' he says. 'My father has forbidden anyone from giving me credit.' I sent him from the house and turned my back on him. Then, a day later, I summoned him. 'Go to the pawn shop,' I told him, 'and he'll give you jewellery on a promise. The Jew will buy it from you.' So he went to such-and-such a pawn shop taking jewellery on a two-month credit line and sold it to the Jew. Then he brought me the money.

Antonia — And what was your scheme all about then?

Nanna — The jewellery was mine, you see? And when the Jew got his money, he brought it all back to me. Then, after eight days, I sent for the fellow who'd given him the jewellery on credit and told him: 'Have that young man thrown in prison. Swear he was trying to flee without paying.' The order was executed and he was arrested, and before he was let out he had to pay a fine twice over. Innkeepers don't let blow-ins eat on the slate.

Antonia — Up until today, I thought I was pretty canny. I confess, I was an asshole for thinkin so.

Nanna — Movin on. The Carnival was approaching, which is torture and death for three things: poor horses, poor clothes, and poor dandies. There was one of my very own customers who had more good intentions than the means to carry them out. It was right after Christmas when they start goin about with the masks on, first only a few, then they begin multiplying like melons, when you might get five or six of a mornin, then ten, twelve, then whole basketsful, so many you feel you want to chuck em away. So things were just gettin started, when my lover Giorgio sees me and says: 'Aren't you gettin masked up?' 'I'm a housecat,' I tell him, 'and an envious one. I'll leave the masks to the beautiful people and those who have the finery to be fitted up in.' 'This Sunday, I want to see you dressed up in your finest costume,' he says. I was quiet for a bit but then I threw my arms around his neck and said: 'My sweetheart, how do you want to see me dressed up?' He says to me: 'I want to see you on horseback, dressed in your best. I'll get my hands on the Cardinal's filly. His stable master promised it to me.' 'That suits me just fine,' I told him, then I waited about seven days before I decided to get dressed up. Comin back to him the Monday following I said: 'First you must give me stockings and breeches, and so as not to add further expense, you can send me your velvet ones. I'll patch them up and make them presentable. The stockings you can pick up for nothing; one of your doublets will do me well too, once I've had it fitted.' When I'd said this I could see him mullin it over. He was havin doubts about puttin me up to all this foolery. Then I says, 'If you don't want to, then fine. You know what, I don't want to get dressed up anymore.' When I let on to go, he grabbed me. 'Is that all you think of me?' he said. He sent his servant off to gather the goods and the tailor too, who'd fit the clothes for me, and sent for the cloth for my stockings which he had cut and sent to me two days later. He helped me get costumed up, tellin me: 'They're made for you', and when I was dressed up in my male clothes, I let him have a go at me as if I were a boy. 'My love,' I says, 'he who buys the broom must also purchase the handle. I need a pair of velvet shoes.' He didn't have any more money, but he took the ring off his finger and pawned it for the velvet, and gave it to a shoemaker who knew my size, and before you know it I had a pair made. After this I fleeced him for a gold-embroidered silk shirt, literally taking the shirt off his back, then I said: 'Give me your cap and I'll have it decorated myself.' Since he was desperate for me to go with him, he gave his new one and wore one he was goin to hand down to his servant. Anyone who'd seen this fool fuss around me would've said, 'See how they're preparing the Senator!' And on the day itself, I sent him out at five in the mornin to buy a plume for my hat, then I came back to get costumed, and because he came back without a mask from Modena, I sent him back out for the proper one.

Antonia — You could've had him do everything in one trip.

Nanna — I could've, but I didn't want to.

Antonia — Why not?

Nanna — Because it made me feel like a lady. Besides, I was one in name anyway.

Antonia — Did you sleep with him the night before the Carnival?

Nanna — After a thousand entreaties, he got a quick poke. I said to him: 'Tomorrow night, if you want, you can do it to me twenty times if ten isn't enough.' Next mornin I made him get up before dawn. 'Go and ready the horse,' I said. 'Once I've eaten, I'll saddle up.' He got up and got dressed and set out, going to find the stable master. 'Well, are we all set?' he says when he gets there. The stable master stared at him blankly, not movin to ready the horse. 'Are you out to ruin me?' my lover cries out then. 'Not at all,' the stable master says, 'but the Cardinal loves this horse, and I know what whores are like. They've no respect for the God above, let alone a lowly beast, and I'm not goin to have him brought back here broken-winded. That'll be the end of me.' But my lover begged and prayed so much that finally the stable master gave in. 'Fine. Send someone for the horse. I'll have it saddled.' The master gave his order to the stableboy and my lover sent his manservant to me, who told me the whole sorry tale. We had a good laugh about the whole thing.

Antonia — These servants are the most traitorous creatures. They are their masters' worst enemies.

Nanna — No doubt about it. So we had breakfast. My lover had barely swallowed six mouthfuls before I told him to send the manservant for the horse. So the boy was sent off, but when he came back he was without the horse. 'The stableboy won't give it to me. He says the master wants to speak to you first.' The boy had scarcely finished speaking but he was hit up the side of the head with a plate.

Antonia — Why did his master fling a plate at him?

Nanna — He threw it because the boy'd said all this out loud instead of callin him aside so I couldn't hear. So I squared on my lover and yelled: 'Now I'm right screwed, right screwed indeed... and all because I wanted to have a more beautiful mask than this face my whore of a mother gave me. I thought you were gonna take care of this. I was daft to believe it and let you fill my head with this nonsense. What's worst of all is that folk'll say I was stitched up!' He tried to assure me I'd get the horse but I turned my back on him. 'Get the hell out of my sight!' I told him. After puttin on his cape and flyin off to the stable, he begged the master so much that in the end he got the bloody horse. With every little noise outside I was runnin to the window, until finally the boy ran up sweatin. 'Ma'am, he's on his way.' No sooner had he said it than the horse was dragged around the corner, the manservant cursin the heavens for all the hoppin about the horse was doin. I was hangin clean out the window, so everyone passin by could see who was goin to ride it. All the children gathered around, shoutin: 'This lady here is gettin masked up for the ball!' After the horse came my lover. Very cheerfully he says, 'We must send the men ahead.' Ten fellows were standin by awaitin orders. I gave him a kiss and asked for the velvet robe his manservant was supposed to bring the previous evenin. The cloak hadn't arrived because the sot had forgotten it, and if I hadn't held back his master, the manservant'd never have lifted a hand again. Anyway, he ran off and got it, and I put it on. While I was fixin up my stockings, my eyes fell upon his fancy garters, which I took a shine to, and so I swiped his and gave him mine, which weren't much to write home about. After I was all got up, which took more time than it does to amass a fortune, and after a lot of blowin and puffin, I got up on the horse. Soon as I was up my lover climbed up on his little nag and we went on our way. He wanted all of Rome to see me with him, so he took my hand as we went. We stopped and bought a basket of eggs filled with rose water, which I cast about me willy-nilly, and we set off once more. When we reached the Borgo, which was knee deep in mud, I set off with no care for either the horse or the fine cape I was wearin, and went twice around it at a gallop, leavin my lover behind. I bumped into him later around a half-dozen times, and I barely had the time of day for him, and he'd try to follow me for a bit but could never catch up on his nag. When night came upon us, I sang out with a thousand other whores:

I shiver in the middle of summer,
heart burning for winter...

My lover caught up with me again and snatched at my hand in desperation. So I said goodnight to my company and, with mask in hand, I says to Giorgio: 'For the love of God, where have you been? You left me all alone, and I know why...' The fool was tryin to put the blame on me when we happened upon the Campo di Fiori, and I rode right up to a peddler and took two capons and a whole string of thrushes, handed them to a porter and told Giorgio: 'Pay him!' He was forced to pay with a ruby his mother had given him when he'd come to Rome, which was as precious to him as the parting of it was painful. At my house there were no candles, firewood, bread or wine—I'd made sure of it—so I flew into a rage and only calmed down when he went out to buy them himself, since his manservant had gone to return the horse. The stable master, when he saw the state of the horse, swore he'd never lend him out again, not even if Christ himself was doin the askin. I was flat out in the bed, and had been there a good while when he returned with the stuff. He helped my mother set the table and dinner was ready in the blink of an eye, and just as we were finishing dinner I heard a coughing outside the window. I ran to see; outside was one of my lovers, a merchant, so I rushed out and we went off together, leavin the other at my house all night. He didn't sleep. He paced about the house, shoutin and ballin about what he'd do to me when he got his hands on me. Gettin the cape he'd lent me back off me was like gettin blood from a stone, I can tell ya. His manservant came eight days in a row before I handed it over.

Antonia — Not a very civilised way to act, Nanna, to a man who'd done so much just to spend the night with you.

Nanna — It was civilised in a whorish way. And no less fun than what I treated the sugar merchant to. I traded this man my sugar for his, and while it lasted, we were even sweetenin our salads. And when he got a taste for my sugar, he'd have said his own was bitter as lemons.

Antonia — Yet he still showered you with it.

Nanna — Ha ha! This fella used to go crazy just lookin at my little peach. He'd get wild hard just playin with it, and he'd touch it, rub it, flick it... He said it had a nicer smile than even those marble statues of women you see here and there around Rome. He wasn't wrong—and I don't mean to toot my own horn—for I had a lovely little beaver. It was almost bald and my slit was so tidy you could barely see it. Not too swollen and not too sunken. I swear, the sugar merchant kissed me more on my cooch than he did on the mouth. He even liked to suck on it like a little freshly laid egg.

Antonia — The scallywag.

Nanna — Why scallywag?

Antonia — For the ill God should visit on him.

Nanna — Didn't God condemn him when he made him fall in love with me?

Antonia — Not as much as He should've.

Nanna — Now, I can't relate every tiny little way I stripped my lovers of everything they owned, nor how I did it without their knowledge, since I always spoke with the forked tongue of a whore. So when some dunderhead came to see me, I was able to outsmart him using a whore's code. The noose was around their necks before they even knew it. The tongue of a rascal is worthy only of rascals, since a thousand rascalities are done by it. But now let me tell you how I swindled this fella from Siena. At least I think that's where he was from.

Antonia — He couldn't have come from anywhere else.

Nanna — Anyway, this fella had only just arrived in Rome, and he couldn't take his eyes off me. There wasn't a time when he'd come across my maid that he didn't have something to say: 'This heart of mine belongs to your lady', or some such muck. 'Tell me, my pretty thing, what is your lady doing?' was another. 'My lady does very well, thanks to his lordship,' my maid would reply, then make faces at him behind his back. One day I saw him pacin back and forth outside, so I said to the maid: 'Go down there and ask him for road tax, since he's blockin the way by moseying back and forth all day.' The maid went to the door and shouted: 'Go and break a leg, you hear me! Yes, you! I don't want to see you again, you filthy wretch! Scoundrel!' The scruff replied: 'What's the matter? I'm at your lady's pleasure... I offer only my service, I swear it.' The maid pretended not to understand. 'Four hours... four hours ago I sent that little thief to change a ducat so we

126

could tip the porter for bringin two lengths of crimson satin to my lady, a gift from Prince Twisty Bollocks. He's still not back.' The eejit wanted to be known as a spender, so he pulled out his purse. 'Here, take it... it's for your lady, because I adore her. I adore her!' He put four crowns in her hand, makin a great show of it. Then he whispered to the maid: 'She likes me, right?' The maid called me but I didn't answer, so she shut the door in his face. He lingered there outside, like a wedding guest without an invite tryin to muscle his way in.

Antonia — Madman. He got what was comin to him.

Nanna — But let's get on to the story of the cats.

Antonia — What kind of cats you talkin about, now?

Nanna — I owed a salesman twenty-five ducats. Since I'd no intention of ever givin it to him, I came up with a good way to stiff him. So what'd I do? I had two very beautiful cats. One day, I saw from the window the fellow approaching, so I gave one of the cats to my maid, I took the other, and said to the maid: 'When he comes to the door, I'll shout, "Strangle the bloody thing, damnit!" And you pretend you don't want to. Then I'll make like to choke the one I'm holdin.' As soon as the words were out of my mouth, he showed up.

Antonia — Did he not knock first?

Nanna — No. The door was open, so he let himself on up the stairs. As soon as he was up, I began screamin: 'Strangle it, damnit! Strangle it!' The maid begged me not to make her do it and to forgive the animals, promising they would never again scoff our dinner. I let on I was furious and gripped the cat by the neck, shoutin: 'Never again!' Well, the salesman, seein the two cats, took pity on them and asked me to gift them to him. 'Not a hope,' I told him. 'By your good grace, ma'am, leave them with me for a week. After a week, if you haven't forgiven them and don't want to give them to me, I'll help you kill them myself.' So he took the cats and put them in a sack while I put up a show of resistance. 'Make sure you have them back here in a week,' I said, 'because I'm going to kill the little buggers.' Then he asked me for twenty-five ducats, and I swore I'd bring it to his shop in ten days. He went away reassured. Ten days, fifteen days passed, then he returned and asked me for the money. I had the money in a cloth purse and jingled it. 'Happily,' I said. 'But first I want my cats.' 'What about your cats?' he says. 'They took off over the roof soon as I left them alone in my house!' I knew it had happened before he'd even said it. I frowned and gave him a scolding look. 'You'd better get those cats back here, or it'll cost you more than twenty-five ducats. You promised me, and you'll get em back here if you have to travel to Barbery to get em!' When the man, who was leanin on the window, saw my cries had raised a whole kerfuffle in the street, he shut his gob and ran down the stairs. 'That's what you get for trusting a whore!' he shouted as he fled.

Antonia — Nanna, I wanna tell you somethin I thought.

Nanna — Go on.

Antonia — That little cat prank is so beautiful that for the sweetness of it I figure you'll be forgiven four of your most hellish sins.

Nanna — Think so?

Antonia — I'd bet my soul for a pistachio.

Nanna — That's no small thing. *Achoo!* Oh God, no, I think I'm catchin a chill. *Achoo!* This fig tree has shaded us too well from the sun. Now I won't be able to tell you about all the men I sweet-talked and swindled so deliciously I had em believin the synagogue floated in the air, and that the burial place of Mohammed—*Achoo!* God, I can scarce breathe, I'm almost hoarse.

Antonia — Walnut trees give bad shade, not the fig tree.

Nanna — Come here, give me your opinion like you promised me, cause I'm dyin here. *Achoo!* I feel bad about not bein able to tell you more. You know, with my lovers, I pretended to go easy on their purses, and didn't like my men to go about all in fancy get-up and throw big banquets. But that was all so the money was saved for my appetites, and these nitwits praised me for my discretion, all while I was robbin em blind. Oh, God save me, I'm croakin!

Antonia — Go on, tell me one more Nanna. Just for me. Come on!

Nanna — Well, there was this gentle— a fellow, a man, you see... Oh for God's sake, help me spit it out! Forgive me, sweetheart, I'll have to tell you another time. And I'll even tell you about the monsignor who ran spank-arsed across the roofs of the district... Oh Christ, Antonia, I feel faint... *Achoo!*

Antonia — Curses on the sun for interrupting our chat. You know, I didn't want to say it earlier, but I didn't believe all those things you saw when you entered the nunnery. Not even that you let the Bachelor take you that very first day.

Nanna — I'm tellin you, when I became a nun I was only half virgin. And as for seein so many mad things in a single day, I can tell you, I've seen far, far worse... *Hch!* Damn this cough!

Antonia — You've got it bad, Nanna.

Nanna — Aye. But will you tell me your opinion like you promised?

Antonia — To get back to that promise I made, I can't keep it.

Nanna — Eh! Why not?

Antonia — Because I meant it when I said it. But since we women are wise without thinking and daft after giving somethin thought, I'll give you my opinion. You can take the rose and fling away the thorns.

Nanna — Go on.

Antonia — I say that chucking some of what you said and takin the rest on your word, that lies are always mixed with truth and sometimes stories are fleshed out to make them more fun—

Nanna — So you take me for a li—*Achoo!*—for a liar?

Antonia — Not a liar, no. Just a little neglectful of the truth. I think you have it in for the nuns and for married women for some other thing. I grant you, there are more bad ones among em than there should be. As for the whores, I can take or leave em.

Nanna — I don't—*Achoo!*—know how to answer, and I'm afraid this cough is gonna floor me. So go on quickly and give me your advice.

Antonia — I say you advise Pippa to become a whore. A nun only betrays her vows, and a wife shits on the sanctity of marriage. A whore violates neither church nor husband. She's like a soldier, who does what she's paid to do. And even if she does evil, she's only sellin what her shop stocks; when a tavernkeeper opens an inn, he doesn't put up a sign—everyone knows there'll be eatin, drinkin, gamblin, cheatin and screwin within, and no one goes there to find fasting or say prayers, for they'll find neither lent nor an altar. Farmers sell vegetables, an apothecary drugs, and the whorehouses sell blasphemies, lies, gibberish, scandal, dishonesty, thievery, filth, hatred, cruelty, the clap, treachery, a bad name, poverty and death. But because a confessor is like a doctor who'd quicker heal the evil that shows itself on your body than the unseen one, with Pippa, make a whore of her right off. After, go and make a little petition, and with two drops of holy water you'll clean the whorishness right outta her. Secondly, from what you've said, I reckon a whore's vices are really virtues. It's a fine thing to be called a lady, dressing well and always feasting and goin to weddings, as you know better than I do. What matters more is scratchin every itch, and feelin the pleasure of each one, because Rome always was and always will be a whore's town.

Nanna — You speak well, Antonia. I'm gonna do just as you advise me.

With that they woke the maid, who was sleeping next to them all the while, and the maid put the basket on her head and took the flask in hand, and Antonia lifted up the tablecloth and they all went home. Antonia sent out for some medicine for Nanna and they dined that evening together, then she stayed the night, and in the morning she returned to her little store, the small business where she spent her life and by which she kept her head above water. Poverty was hard on Antonia but Nanna's words gave her some comfort, and she was amazed at the evil whores wrought in this world, whom there were more of than all the mosquitoes of twenty summers. And she hadn't even heard the half of it.

Many thanks to Kindra.

Epigraph from Susan Sontag, *Partisan Review*, 1967.

Meat

In the murky wake of the financial crisis a string of establishments pop up across Europe catering to a hedonistic underground, its clientele beholden to a strange, hallucinatory meat. Stoked by the fleshy and charismatic Hugo and fuelled by voracious consumption of ecstasy, the craze spreads from the heart of Europe all the way to the Mediterranean, where in Athens the financial elite begin to turn on each other. Murder, barbecue and apocalyptic raving ensues, culminating in the most savage party Mykonos has ever seen. Follow the story to its destructive end, where consumption eats itself alive.

Notes from a Cannibalist

1847. Assuming the identity of a dead Jesuit priest, a survivor of the famine in Ireland travels to South America where he is tasked with rebuilding the missions among the natives. Inducted into local life, Father James Carmichael finds love with a native woman and becomes acquainted with the ways of the Guaraní, discovering ayahuasca and ritualism. In a battle with his own gods and demons, the priest fights for the life he envisions, his own self the ultimate stake of the struggle. Worlds are shattered, realities crumbled, lives destroyed. His soul victim to the crucible of the New World, what is tempered in the chaos will be outside his control.

A Whore's Song

Hidden away in the backstreets of Amsterdam is a secretive whorehouse, open only to those in the know, where torture, pain and extreme sexual sport are the vehicle to understanding and self-knowledge. Run by the obscure Madame Zhu, the establishment is a magnet to the city's elite and mad soul-seekers alike. Two lives collide in a chaotic downward spiral brought about by psychoactives and sexual torture when, over the course of a day, a whore recounts her life as a destroyer of egos and one man is forced to face his deepest demons. Cast out into the far reaches of his mind, will he make it back from the other side?

In a world where the weak become prey and strength means brutality, living may come at the cost of dying first.

The Book of God

God isn't dead. He's just a bit mental...

Indignant at his corrupt and ignominious creation, God sits and stews in his treehouse outside the small town of Brawl. His only companion and sole remaining attendant, a withered and tortured scribe, chronicles the Lord's descent into madness as he struggles to collect all the lost souls which have escaped his records and further addled the Lord's already woolly mind. But when the Scribe is forced to hire a maid to care for the Almighty, the introduction of a buxom woman into God's life brings chaos in its wake. And what's more, the maid has an innocent and attractive young daughter...

Suffering rejection, humiliation and loathing of humankind, God seeks a way to bring back Christ and trigger the Apocalypse. The only thing standing in his way? God's old harpy of a mother...

The Jaguar

1849. Salome Azul, daughter of a powerful politician, flees Buenos Aires at the height of the Argentinian civil war. In London she enlists the help of Irishman Sean Ryan to open The Nightingale, a high-class brothel and opium den that will be used to entrap and blackmail London's political elite.

In doing so she will make enemies. What's more, Ms. Azul has carried her own demons from Argentina, and it is these that will prove her most relentless foe.

In order to survive, she must eliminate all weakness from her character. Doing so may mean cutting away all she cherishes most.

In the pursuit of power, unrelenting sacrifice is what decides who lives and dies.

Little Swine

A small basement cell. A dirty bed. A chair.

These are the confines of Little Swine's world. Prisoner of Momma and subject to the tortures of Boy, her life is a living hell.

Momma is a disturbed woman. Her plan is simple: Momma wants a baby so that she may redeem the sins of her past. This is Little Swine's purpose. And when Momma has what she wants, Little Swine will be discarded.

But violence gives way to violence and blood begets blood, and many will die before the devil has his quota. One can never underestimate the power of retribution.

The Cottage

Men are men until they encounter evil. And after, they are compelled to do evil itself.

Turning their backs on New York, John and Katie Mears purchase their dream home in colonial Connecticut, the place they hope to raise their firstborn and build life as a family. But the cradle of the American nation has a haunting past, and they find themselves swallowed by a dark history, one of blood and anguish, a specter of the country's painful birth in the slaughter of pilgrim times. The dark crucible of the nation is yet manifest. Blood debt is eternal, and sooner or later history calls for retribution. It is the blood of innocents that pays for the sins of the father.

The Sistema Series

There is a company that provides a deeply sinister service for shady clients: subconscious torture for political or corporate manipulation. Vangelis Zervas is an agent of Vathos and does his job with zero qualms. But when a young boy is killed over a highly coveted piece of software that may have been produced by the company, the boy's mother goes in search of her son's killers. Meeting a group of disparate rebels with their own hostility toward Vathos, they join forces to bring down the company. Vangelis Zervas is on their radar, but will he see his way to help them and go rogue, or stay true to the devil inside?

Sistema is a dystopian/cyberpunk horror that journeys into hell itself in exploration of man's search for power and control.